D1311068

Six are they, the Badgers' Crowns

If power ye seek, they must be found

Crystal, iron and flaming fire

Gather them, if ye desire

Ice, and wood and carven stone

The power they give

Is yours

Alone

SUNDERED LANDS

THE ICEGATE OF SPYRE

BY ALLAN FREWIN JONES
AND GARY CHALK

ILLUSTRATIONS BY

GARY
CHALK

Hodder
Children's
Books

A division of Hachette Children's Books

First published in Great Britain in 2011
by Hodder Children's Books

1

A Catalogue record for this book is available from the British Library

ISBN 978 0 340 98812 1

Typeset by Avon DataSet Ltd, Bidford on Avon, Warwickshire
Printed and bound by CPI Bookmarque Ltd, Croydon, Surrey

The paper and board used in this paperback by Hodder Children's Books
are natural recyclable products made from wood grown in sustainable
forests. The manufacturing processes conform to the environmental
regulations of the country of origin.

Hodder Children's Books
A division of Hachette Children's Books
338 Euston Road, London NW1 3BH
An Hachette UK company
www.hachette.co.uk

Prologue

The legends say that once, long, long ago, there was a single round world, like a ball floating in space, and that it was ruled over by six wise badgers. The legends also tell of a tremendous explosion, an explosion so huge that it shattered the round world into a thousand fragments, a vast archipelago of islands adrift in the sky. As time passed, the survivors of the explosion thrived and prospered and gave their scattered island homes a name – and that name was the Sundered Lands.

That's what the legends say.

But who believes in legends nowadays?

Well . . . Esmeralda Lightfoot, the Princess in Darkness, does, for one. According to Esmeralda, the truth of the ancient legends was revealed to her in a reading of the Magical and Ancient Badger Blocks – a set of prophetic wooden tokens from the Old Times. And her companions are beginning to believe it as well: reluctant hero Trundle Boldoak, light-hearted minstrel Jack Nimble, and the loopy ex-pirate Ishmael March have all joined in the quest, and they've already found three of the crowns.

But there is a problem. Someone else is also hunting for the six crowns – his name is Captain Grizzletusk, and he's the meanest, bloodthirstiest, wickedest pirate ever to sail the skies of the Sundered Lands. And just to make matters even worse, Grizzletusk and his murderous pirate band are being helped by none other than Millie Rose Thorne – Esmeralda's very own aunty!

For the moment, our heroes have outrun their pursuers – but if they think their problems are over, they're about to find out they have another think coming!

Land, Ho!

'Can I wear the crown again yet?' asked Ishmael, twisting his ears between his paws and looking at his three companions with big, mournful eyes.

'No,' Esmeralda replied, for the tenth time. 'The Crown of Fire is staying safe and sound in its biscuit tin.'

Trundle gazed sympathetically at the loony ship's cook. Ishmael seemed so sad, sitting there forlornly in the narrow prow of *The Thief in the Night*.

'Never you mind, old pal,' said Jack, perching on the skyboat's rail at Ishmael's side and lightly running his bow across the strings of his rebec. 'Let me cheer you up with a merry ditty.'

'Rattle me bones and strain me gravy,' sighed Ishmael, his long head between his paws. 'Even an oyster has his wheelbarrow, and that's a fact!'

Trundle did feel sorry for the poor old chap. It wasn't so very long ago that the loopy hare had been strutting around in the ruins of the phoenix nest, the beautiful fiery crown jammed on to his head, spouting out clues for the next stage of their quest.

'This clue you have found in the phoenix bird's fire
You must seek for the Crown of Ice in the land
of Spyre!'

Trundle had never heard of Spyre, but Jack had a

pretty good idea of how to get there. The carefree musician had been everywhere and seen everything. Sometimes Trundle felt quite inadequate, remembering his quiet, dull, little life on the windswept flats of Shiverstones, with its acres and acres of dismal, depressing cabbages. Although his life hardly lacked for excitement since he had met up with Esmeralda!

'Here's a little song I've written about our adventures,' said Jack, as he stroked his bow across a block of rosin so it would play smoothly. 'I call it "A Quester's Life". I hope you like it.' He cleared his throat, attacked the strings with the bow and began to sing:

Oh, a quester's life is a jolly life, although it may
be short
We're on the run; it's lots of fun, with a foe in
every port

Even dear old Aunty Millie makes our life quite fraught

And we'll hang on high 'neath the starry sky, if by

pirates we are caught

Ohhhhh, we'll hang on high and must say goodbye,

if by pirates we are caught.

'I'm sorry,' interrupted Trundle. 'Is that supposed to cheer us up? Because if it is, then you've seriously misjudged your audience.'

Jack frowned at him, his bow falling still. 'Everyone's a critic these days,' he sighed.

Trundle got up and made his way to the stern of the skyboat, where Esmeralda was busy at the tiller. It was a bonny, breezy day, and the skies of Sundered Lands were full of fluffy white clouds. Dotted above and below and behind and in front were scores of distant floating islands. Some were mountainous, others flat and barren; some sported large towns and cities, shining like jewels, others were all farmland and rolling hills or deep forests and tumbling silvery waterfalls.

Occasionally a windship would pass close by and Trundle would wave at the sailors in the rigging – and sometimes they would wave back as they went on their way. At such times, he would shiver with the delight of being out here in the wide worlds, experiencing all the remarkable wonders of the Sundered Lands. And then sometimes he would think of the pirates who were chasing them, and of Esmeralda's treacherous Aunt Millie – and his hand would stray to the hilt of his newfound sword and he would wish he were back home again, with a stout oak door between him and all their troubles.

'How far to Spyre now?' he asked Esmeralda.

'A hop and a skip,' she declared. 'We'll be there before nightfall, if the skycharts are accurate.'

'They have been so far,' Trundle said, leaning over to look at the unrolled chart that was spread out at her feet. 'I just wish they could tell us a bit more about the place we're going to.' He frowned, turning to the great heap of provisions and gear that filled the rear of the skyboat. 'There's a whole bunch of papers and documents in there. Shall I go and see if any of them mention Spyre?'

'By all means, if it'll make you happy,' chirruped Esmeralda.

Trundle smiled. 'You're in a very good mood today.'

'And why not!' Esmeralda replied. 'We've seen no sign of Captain Grizzletusk for days on end, we've outfoxed my wicked aunty, plus we've already found three of the six crowns, to boot. I think we can feel pretty proud of ourselves, Trundle, my lad!'

She had a point. Half the crowns had been

discovered. The first two – the Crowns of Crystal and Iron – were in the ancient city of Widdershins, in the keeping of their friend the Herald Persuivant, while the third – the Crown of Fire – was safely stowed away in an old biscuit tin under Esmeralda's seat.

Yes, all in all, she had good reason to be feeling cheerful. Things were going marvellously well. Trundle wrinkled his forehead. Oh, dear. That was just the kind of thinking that could jinx the whole quest! He cleared his head of over-confident thoughts and busied himself rummaging among their provisions. Surely there would be *something* useful among all this stuff?

'Aha!' he crowed, pulling a rolled-up scroll from the pile and brandishing it in the air.

Written in an ornate style on the outside of the scroll were the words:

The Ingenious and Instructive Guide for
Pleasant Relaxings and Spiritual Illuminatings
on the Pilgrim Island of Spyre

'What have you found?' asked Jack.

Trundle sat down and unrolled the scroll. 'It's some kind of guide,' he said. Across the top of the scroll was written the following, in large, decorated letters:

Spyre! The Perfection of Pilgrimage Destinations –
whether your seekings are Enlightenment
or Relaxation
or Just Plain Good Timings

There was something very odd about the way this guide had been written – and it only got stranger as more of the script was revealed.

Jack came and perched behind Trundle, reading aloud.

'*Special Offer*,' he pronounced, '*partake of two vouchers for free tea at Rachette Chop-Chop's Magnanimous Rissole Restaurant. (Vegetarian option.)*' He rubbed his snout with a paw. 'Hmm. Sounds a good deal – we should take them up on that.'

'Take a look ahead,' came Esmeralda's excited voice from the stern. 'Spyre, ho, my hearties!'

Trundle and Jack lifted their heads from the scroll.

'Lawks!' exclaimed Jack, his eyes bulging.

'Crikey!' gasped Trundle, open-mouthed.

'Ahoy, Cap'n, there be giblets in the wind!' warbled Ishmael, his ears knotting and unknotting themselves rapidly.

They had good reason to be astonished.

Spyre was a very astonishing island.

At first glance and in the distance it looked to Trundle like a great, elongated teardrop hanging in the sky, green at the base and sparkling white at the point. Fascinated and thrilled, he snatched up the skyboat's telescope and applied it to his eye.

'According to this guide there are thick impenetrable jungles and slimy swamps at the bottom of Spyre,' said Jack. 'We'll want to steer clear of that region.'

'Yes. I see them!' Trundle roved the telescope up the curiously-shaped island. There was more greenery above the jungles and swamps, but it looked neater – more like cultivated fields.

And then came something truly odd: some kind of barrier had been built above the green fields, circling the island like the brim of a hat.

Above that, Trundle saw a whole mass of buildings: a thriving town, by the look of it. On terraces above the town were the coral-coloured walls and roofs of what he took to be a huge, sprawling castle. And then, far above both town and castle, towered the peaks and pinnacles and crests of a huge, snow-covered mountain.

'Wow,' Trundle said. 'Amazing!'

'Hey, Ishmael – take over the tiller, there's a good fellow,' called Esmeralda. 'I want to take a look at that guide.'

'Sure as ninepins, your ladyshipness,' chortled Ishmael, clambering over the provisions heap and relieving her in the stern. 'Trust old Ishmael, he won't steer ye wrong.'

'See that you don't!' warned Esmeralda. She came up behind Trundle and Jack amidships. 'Give us a lend of that telescope, Trun,' she said. Trundle handed it over and for the next few minutes they took turns in getting a close-up view of the rapidly approaching island.

'So? What else does that guide tell us?' asked Esmeralda.

The three of them huddled over the guide. The writing was smaller now, and they had to lean in close to read it.

The Island of Spyre are divided into four regions, the guide informed them. *At the bottom is bad place we don't go – not for pilgrims!*

'Why is it written in such a peculiar way?' Trundle wondered aloud.

'The population of Spyre comes from all over the Sundered Lands,' Jack explained. 'Not everyone speaks the Common Tongue. There are dozens of different languages in the Sundered Lands – you just haven't been to any places where they're spoken.'

'Oh, I see,' said Trundle, feeling a little ignorant and deciding to be more tolerant of the guide's strange style.

Above bad places is the extensive tea-plantings of Lowspace, he read, *where delicious beverage is grown for drinkings home and abroad. Then pilgrims will see Boardwall, where the pilgrim zone begin. Above this is teeming metropolis of Downtown, and it is here that all pilgrims will moor and find good feedings and beddings and helpful guides in plenty.*

'Ishmael, keep a weather eye out, there's a good fellow,' Esmeralda called, her eyes still fixed on the scroll.

'No problems!' Ishmael called back.

Pilgrims will then be in friendly and hospitable

parts of Spyre and ready to take tour to the famous and legendary monasteries, where mystical Lamas dwell and ruminate on secrets of the world all day and night, mostly.

'I've heard of the Lamas of Spyre,' said Jack. 'They're supposed to be totally awesome!'

The Lamas of Spyre are happy to give out words of wisdom and enlightenment, and free Badger Block readings, too, for those pilgrims who have paid for the Special Deluxe Thousand Steps to Radiant Wisdom Tour (tips accepted with much thankings). Tours available for all pockets – from budget trips to all-in extravagants!

'I'm not sure I like the sound of a deluxe tour,' muttered Trundle. 'I bet it'll be really expensive.'

'Oh, live a little, Trundle!' said Esmeralda. 'We can afford it. Besides, we have to land here to search for the Crown of Ice – so we might as well make the most of it.'

'My thinking exactly,' agreed Jack. 'And look what it says here.' He read aloud: '*Stairways lead up from the monasteries to specially constructed Enlightenment Platforms where lucky pilgrims can see the legendary Ice Gate of Spyre. This is most mystical and wondrous sight in all of Sundered Lands. Enlightenment guaranteed or your money back.*'

Jack grinned. 'Well, you can't say fairer than that.'

'Hey, Ishmael,' called Esmeralda. 'How are we doing?'

'Fine as a ferret,' Ishmael replied cheerfully. 'No problems!'

'You'll let us know when we get close, won't you?' called Esmeralda.

'Sure thing, I will, your nobilitiness!'

'So, what's the plan?' asked Trundle.

'We make landfall in Downtown,' Esmeralda said. 'We probably have funds enough for the all-in tour, plus a bit left over for emergencies.' She beamed at her two companions. 'And then we let the Fates show us the way to the Crown of Ice!'

'Sounds dandy to me,' said Jack. He tapped the scroll. 'But you should cast an eye over this bit.'

Warnings to all pilgrims, read Trundle and Esmeralda. *Downtown is only safe place to land, trust us. Why we lie to you, honoured guest? Swampy jungles full of dangerous beastlies and high snow-slopes of mountain is where deadly albino snow snakes live. Even baby snakes are ten foot long and adults can swallow entire windship in one gulp. Very nasty!*

'That's worth knowing,' said Esmeralda.

'With our luck, the Crown of Ice is going to be right in the middle of all those snakes,' sighed Trundle.

'Oh, don't be such a Gloomy Gus,' said

Esmeralda. 'Hey, Ishmael?' she called over her shoulder. 'How's it going?'.

'Sweet as a swannicle!'

'Don't let us get too close before you give me a call,' she warned.

'Leave it to old Ishmael, he knows a shrimp from a serving hatch, so he does!'

'So, that's the plan,' Jack said. 'Landfall in Downtown, stop off for a tasty meal and a good night's kip. Then we take a leisurely stroll up to the monasteries – at which point we put our trust in Esmeralda's Fates to steer us right.' He gave them a toothy grin. 'Spiffy! What could possibly go wrong?'

About half a second after Jack had finished speaking, Trundle got the distinct impression that the whole world was coming to an end.

Crash! Crunch! Bash! Wallop! Thud!

He felt himself turning head over heels while

his two friends and the entire contents of *The Thief in the Night* went flying around his ears like shrapnel.

Smash! Crack! Wham! Whack! Splinter!

Trundle was vaguely aware of branches and leaves and vines and lianas whizzing past as he was thrown through the air like a rag doll. When at last the chaos and the noise and the mayhem and the spinning around came to a sudden, shuddering halt, he found himself clinging desperately to the branch of a tree with his feet dangling in thin air. Spitting out fragments of leaf, he peered frantically down between his waggling toes.

He was in the topmost branches of a very tall tree. Way, way down, he could just about make out the green and swampy-looking ground.

A muffled voice called out from somewhere above him. It was Ishmael, sounding rather pleased with himself.

'Land ho!' he announced.

Bats!

'Good evening,' said a friendly voice. 'How very jolly of you to drop in.'

Trundle blinked and found himself staring into the upside-down face of a large, smiling bat.

'Umm . . .' His brain was spinning like a top inside his skull.

'We so seldom get visitors,' continued the bat. 'Could I persuade you to partake of a nice cup of tea?'

Trundle took a deep breath and closed his eyes,

waiting for his brain to stop revolving. When he opened them again, the cheerful bat was still peering quizzically at him – the right way up now.

He also noticed other things. Like the fact that *The Thief in the Night* was wedged in the branches of the tree a few yards above him – upside down with its mast snapped in two and its sail in shreds and its propeller broken and all their provisions gone. A few bits and pieces of their gear hung like peculiar fruit in the tree, but Trundle presumed the rest lay smashed and splattered way down on the jungle floor.

A short way off, Esmeralda was jammed in a fork between two branches, struggling to free herself. Jack was clinging to the remains of the mast, his precious rebec clutched in one hand. Their steersman had got himself stuck feet-upwards in a tangle of branches with a flour sack over his head.

The only *comforting* thing Trundle noticed was

that the biscuit tin with the Crown of Fire in it was trapped under the stern seat – so at least *that* had survived the wreck!

'Ups-a-daisy,' chortled the bat, helping Trundle down on to the relative safety of a wide branch. 'That was quite a tumble you folk took. Trainee steersman, was it?'

'Something like that,' gasped Trundle, straightening his clothes and making sure his sword was all right.

Several other bats were climbing through the tree, helping Esmeralda and Jack and Ishmael out of their precarious positions and dusting them off. Once everyone was the right way up and feeling a little better, and the box with the crown in it had been retrieved, Esmeralda spent quite a while telling Ishmael exactly what she thought of him. Trundle was amazed that anyone could yell for so long without taking a breath. And all the while, Ishmael was grinning and nodding enthusiastically and saying things like: 'That's the way! You tell it like it is, ma'am! Don't you hold back!' until Trundle was sure he saw steam coming out of Esmeralda's ears.

'You addle-pated, woolly-headed, bone-bonced, thick-skulled, pea-brained nincompoop!' Esmeralda finished, finally running out of breath.

'Encore!' shouted Ishmael, applauding loudly. 'Bravo! *Bravissimo!*'

Esmeralda let out a scream like a kettle coming to the boil and had to be restrained by Jack from hitting Ishmael over the head with the biscuit tin.

Trundle gazed around at this new environment. The upper branches of the huge jungle tree were hung with odd-looking little dwelling places, linked by narrow stairways and bridges. These treehouses were made from dark wood and were very thin and crooked

and pointy and angular, with high-
arched doors and windows that
glowed with a warm
red light.

In the distance,
similar lights burned in
other trees, flaring in the
gloom of the gathering
evening. This part of the
jungle was obviously
home to quite a
sizeable clan of the
large bats.

'Well, we can't stay
here,' Esmeralda said, after taking a few
long, slow breaths to help her calm down. '*The
Thief in the Night* is a total wreck, of course. We'll
have to abandon her. It's a long climb down, but we'll

salvage what we can and make our way out of here on foot.' She glared daggers at Ishmael. 'Thanks to you, *nitwit*!'

'Many a mickle makes a mackerel,' Ishmael remarked.

'Oh – shut up!'

'Pardon me,' said the first bat. 'I really wouldn't go down to the ground if I were you. That's not a good idea at all.'

'We have to get to Downtown,' said Jack. 'We're on an important quest.'

'How thrilling!' said a second bat. 'But the night is drawing on, and the beasts will soon be waking up.'

'And if you go down there,' the first bat added, pointing groundwards and shuddering, 'you'll get eaten all up right down to your toe-bones.'

'Yes, that's right,' chorused more bats,

gathering around them. 'They'll chew you up and spit out the gristle. It's what they do, those beastly beasts!'

'They eat the flowers of the dark lotus plant,' said the first bat. 'And the dark lotus does fearful things to even the most sweet-natured of folk!'

'It drives them out of their minds,' said bat

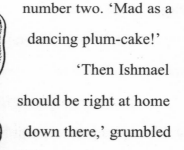

number two. 'Mad as a dancing plum-cake!'

'Then Ishmael should be right at home down there,' grumbled Esmeralda. She eyed the bats. 'Are the beasts really that dangerous?'

'At night they are,' said the first bat. 'But they sleep during the day, so you'd probably be safe once the sun comes up again.'

'Spend the night up here with us,' suggested

another of the bats. 'You can set off at first light.'

'And you could have a nice cup of tea before you bed down,' said another.

'Yes – our special tea,' said yet another.

'Our special tea is our specialty,' chorused the rest. 'Oh, please, don't go! We so seldom have guests. Please stay!'

Trundle and Esmeralda and Jack looked at one another.

'Oh, why not!' said Esmeralda. 'I could just do with a nice cup of tea, as it happens. But we need to be up and away first thing!'

'Ouch!' grumbled Trundle, wriggling under his blanket. 'Stoppit!' Something was tickling his neck just under his right ear. And he had been so happy and cosy, dreaming pleasant dreams about cream buns and feather beds. He had quite forgotten that he was sleeping in a bat-house in the top of a jungle tree. Being woken by some dratted insect nipping at his neck was just too much.

'Don't wake up,' whispered a voice close to his head. 'Nothing's going on.'

'Eh?' Trundle turned over, to meet the round amber eyes of one of the bats. He blinked a couple of times, gazing in a puzzled and sleepy way at the creature's mouth, which hung open to reveal a pair of long white fangs with drops of blood on their tips.

'Oi! What are you up to?' Trundle yelled, pushing the bat away. He put a paw to his neck and felt two little puncture marks. 'Were you drinking my blood?'

'No, of course not,' said the bat, wiping its mouth. 'The very idea!'

'Yes, you were!' howled Trundle. He took a mighty breath. 'Help! Help – vampire bats! Dirty great

28

blood-sucking vampire bats!' And with that, he leaped out of bed, grabbed his sword and waved it at the disappointed-looking creature.

'Don't be like that,' the bat said. 'We're not greedy. We only want half a cup of fresh blood from each of you. Just to flavour the tea!'

'Fiends!' Trundle heard Esmeralda shout from a nearby house. 'Fiendish blood-sucking fiends!'

'De-fang me, you cad!' Jack roared from another part of the tree.

'A curse on your poultry old bean-bag!' hooted Ishmael. 'That's my favourite throat you're chewing on!'

Trundle poked his sword at the retreating bat. 'Get back, you monster!' he shouted indignantly. 'You'll get no more blood out of us. It's an outrage – feasting on guests, indeed! I've never heard the like!'

A bat came somersaulting out of Esmeralda's

house and want crashing away down the tree. She emerged, dusting her hands together. 'Time to get out of here, folks!' she said. 'Beastly beasties are better than bloodthirsty bats!'

'I'm terribly sorry about the inconvenience,' said Trundle's bat. 'But the simple fact is . . .' and his eyes shone with a dangerous orange light, 'we . . . need . . . blood!'

And all of a sudden the tree was filled with staring orange eyes as the dark and shambling bats came swarming in from every direction.

'We . . . need . . . blood!' they chorused.

'Not on your nelly!' Jack cried. He grabbed Ishmael by the collar and scrambled over to where Trundle was standing, still waving his sword. A couple of moments later, Esmeralda had also joined them.

The bats were closing in. 'We . . . need . . . blood . . . ' they all sang out.

'Down we go!' announced Esmeralda, and without further ado, the four companions began a frantic and hectic descent of the tree.

'Don't go!' howled the bats, climbing down after them, and getting a bit too close for Trundle's liking.

'We . . . need . . . blood!' they sang out. 'We . . . need . . . *blood*!'

3

The Dark Lotus

Thinking about it later, Trundle was amazed that he
and his friends didn't break their necks, the way they
went hurtling down that tree. But fortunately it offered
plenty of handholds on branches and hanging vines
which they were able to grab as they flung themselves
downwards, the bloodthirsty bats racing after them.

Trundle wondered at first why the wicked
creatures didn't simply take to the wing to catch up
with them, but he quickly realized that there were far

too many obstacles in the way. Any bat trying to fly would have crashed into the tangled branches.

As they drew closer to the ground, the bats became fewer and fewer, until only one remained, goggling dejectedly down at them. 'Aww!' it shouted. 'No fair! Come back, tasty guests. Don't go getting eaten by beasties! It'll be such a waste of good blood. Come back!'

'Flap off, fang-face!' called Trundle as he clambered down off the final branch and dropped lightly on to soft, mossy ground.

The others came plopping down around him.

'Well, here's a fine pickle!' Esmeralda stared at the others. 'Who's got the crown?'

There was an awkward silence, broken by Ishmael.

'An empty vessel gathers no moss,' he said, helpfully.

'We *were* in a bit of a rush,' Trundle said

unhappily, remembering that the precious biscuit tin had been in his possession when he had gone to sleep.

'Oh, marvellous!' groaned Esmeralda. 'Well, it can't be helped. And we can't go back up for it now. I'm sure the Fates will show us how to retrieve it later.' She patted Trundle on the shoulder to let him know she didn't blame him. 'So? Anyone see any beasties?'

They all stood very still – hardly even breathing as they stared through the jungle for any sign of movement in the deep darkness.

'There's no smoke without weasels!' Ishmael said loudly.

'Will you pipe down,' growled Esmeralda. 'Do you want every beast for ten miles to hear you?'

'What's that over there?' asked Trundle. He pointed away through the great tree-trunks. 'It looks like lights.'

'Ohhhh yeeeeessss,' breathed Esmeralda. 'Kind of purplie-mauvie-violetie lights. I see them.'

'A town perhaps?' suggested Jack. 'Full of civilized people who don't bite a chap in his sleep?'

'Or full of fearsome beasties who will eat us up to our toe-bones,' Trundle observed.

'I'm not at all sure there are any beasties,' said Esmeralda. 'I think those dratted bats made them up to keep us in their tree. Come on, everyone – let's go check it out. Jack, keep an eye on Ishmael. He's a pain in the prickles, but I wouldn't want him to go wandering off and fall in a swamp.'

They set off towards the light, Trundle taking the lead with his sword ready – just in case the beasts were real. He advanced cautiously, his eyes constantly scanning the jungle for any glimpse of savage beasts. Not a peep. If there were any beasts at all, they must have been busy somewhere else.

It wasn't long before they found themselves heading down into a long, steep, narrow valley. The violet lights were dead ahead, glowing a little eerily in the deep dark jungle night. As they approached, it became obvious that these were not the lights of a town at all; in fact, the weird gleam came from the large hanging flowerheads of a colony of tall purple plants.

'Uh-oh!' murmured Jack. 'I think these are dark lotus plants. We'd better not get too close. Remember what those bats told us – eating them drives people crazy.'

'I hardly think we're going to stop off for a petal sandwich,' said Esmeralda.

'You can't believe everything you read in rooks,' Ishmael remarked.

'I don't fancy climbing all the way up that hill again,' Trundle added. 'And there's no other way forward. Look – there's a path through the flowers! We'll be fine.'

Esmeralda picked up a long stick from the ground. 'If any plant tries to give us a hard time, I'll whack it on the stamen!'

Forming a line, they began to make their way through the towering ranks of the purple-petalled flowers.

Trundle wrinkled his nose. There was a musty and mouldy smell in the air. He heard rustlings and creakings. The looming plants leaned over them, their petals like fleshy lips, their leaves twitching like thin fingers.

'I'm not sure this was such a very good idea after all,' he said. 'Perhaps we ought to go back.'

'Oh dear,' said Jack, looking over his shoulder. 'I'm not sure we can.'

They all looked back. The plants had moved,

blocking the pathway behind them.

'Oh, no you don't, you weirdo weeds!' exclaimed Esmeralda. She hefted the stick in her two paws and gave the nearest of the dark lotus plants a hefty swipe right across the side of its flower.

The rustling and creaking grew louder as fine purple pollen came raining down over the four companions from the head of the walloped flower.

'Not sure that was a great idea,' Jack said uneasily.

Half-blinded by the pollen and sneezing frantically as it filtered into his snout, Trundle blundered about, waving his sword randomly and yelling. 'Get your filthy fronds off me, you perfidious plants! Have at you! Have at . . . have at-*atchoo*!'

He was aware of the voices of the others, yelling as they stumbled this way and that, coughing and sneezing and flailing their arms about to try and fend off the drifting pollen.

And then he lumbered head-first into something hard and solid and all the violet lights went out with a bang!

Trundle found himself wandering aimlessly through the tall dark lotus plants. It was still night-time, but a gleam on the horizon suggested the sun would soon be up. The others were there as well – but they were behaving in a very odd fashion.

Esmeralda was racing madly around and around a tree-trunk, flapping her arms and laughing her head off at nothing in particular. And Jack was sitting on the ground, bowing his rebec and serenading a passing beetle.

They've both gone quite potty, Trundle observed to himself. *How very sad for them. Still, there's no smoke without weasels, as Ishmael would say*. He paused for a moment. *What a very wise old fellow Ishmael is!* he realized suddenly. *I must mention that to him next time I see him.* 'Oh, lawks!' This final yelp was due to the fact that a whole swarm of murderous pirates had suddenly come pounding towards him through the dark lotus plants, waving cutlasses and firing off pistols and muskets.

They were pouring out of a large grey windship that lay at an awkward angle among the trees. With a squawk of alarm, Trundle turned on his tail and legged it at full tilt through the jungle. He swished his sword behind him every now and then, but he could hear the hollering pirates gaining ground. Any second now, they'd be upon him and that would be that.

Curses! he thought. *What a way to go – pummelled to paste by a posse of pesky pirates while my best pals in all of the Sundered Lands have gone stark mad!*

A thin, long-eared figure stepped out in front of him, one paw held up decisively. Trundle skidded to a halt so as not to cannon straight into Ishmael.

'Out of the way!' he screeched. 'The pirates will get us both!'

Ishmael raised an eyebrow. 'There are no pirates, Trundle, dear boy. They're all in your mind.'

'I don't think so,' spluttered Trundle. 'They're all over the jungle – and they're out for blood!' He barged into Ishmael, sending him spinning. 'Run for it!'

A moment later he was aware of Ishmael pattering along beside him. 'Listen to me, Trundle,' said the hare. 'You and Esmeralda and Jack are having hallucinations brought on by that darned pollen. I seem to be the only one completely unaffected by it. Now do pull yourself together, there's a good chap.'

Trundle blinked at him. Ishmael was talking

nonsense! And him being such a sensible fellow, usually. What a terrible shame.

'You're not thinking straight, Ishmael,' he puffed. 'Your mind has been messed up by that dark lotus pollen. I'll look after you, though, never fear. Just keep running!'

Ishmael let out a heavy sigh. 'I'm very sorry, dear boy,' he said. 'But you've gone off your rocker. I obviously need to do something drastic to snap you out of it.'

A firm paw grabbed Trundle by the collar and he was jerked off to one side.

'No! Wait! Stoppit! Leggo!' wailed Trundle as he was dragged unceremoniously through the undergrowth. 'Waddyadoing? We'll be caught by the pirates!' He swivelled around in Ishmael's grip, swinging his sword at the looming pirate hordes.

'My deepest apologies,' said Ishmael. 'Just

remember – this is for your own good.'

Trundle felt himself spun around. He saw a great stretch of brown swampy water right in front of him. He teetered on the bank for a moment, windmilling his arms. A hand gave him a hefty shove in the small of the back. He lost balance and, with a howl, toppled face-first into the water.

Splish! Splash! Sploosh!

'Urgggle!' spluttered Trundle, floundering in the thick brown water. 'Guggle! Gurrg! Ptooie!' He glared up at Ishmael. 'You big twit!' he yelled. 'What did you do that for?'

But before Ishmael had a chance to answer, the pirates reached the soggy swamp and began one by one to leap and jump and dive into the water, laughing and shouting and sending up great spouts of dirty spray that half-swamped poor Trundle.

And then, as if marauding pirates weren't

enough, Esmeralda's Aunt Millie came thundering to the brink of the swamp, leaped on high, wrapped her arms around her shins and came cannonballing into the depths like a great big sack of doorknobs.

Trundle's head disappeared under Aunt Millie's tidal wave.

Doomed to die in a filthy jungle swamp, he thought as the water engulfed him. *What a miserable way to go! Farewell cruel worlds! Farewell!*

Back to Normal

Trundle lifted his snout above the water, coughing and spitting. He gazed around, entirely befuddled. Apart from the odd water-snail clinging to his prickles, he was alone in the swamp. Of the pirates and of Esmeralda's Aunt Millie, there was no sign.

'How very curious!' he gasped, wiping weed out of his eyes and paddling for the bank.

Ishmael had also gone.

'Why, I do believe that clever old hare was

right,' Trundle spluttered. 'My brain was all bunged up with dark lotus pollen. I imagined the whole thing!'

He heard a disturbance in the jungle and a few moments later Ishmael appeared, carrying a struggling Jack by the scruff of his neck and by the seat of his trousers. 'My deepest apologies,' he puffed, bringing Jack to the water's edge and then swinging him back and forth a couple of times to work up some momentum.

'I have to get back to my audience!' howled Jack. 'I was about to give them my rendering of "Advance Ye Voles" with alternative verses.'

'Later, perhaps,' gasped Ishmael as he released the squirming squirrel.

Jack glided in a graceful curve through the air and splashed into the swamp, a few metres away from Trundle.

'Ishmael,' Trundle called, rising and falling on

the seething water. 'I'm in my right mind again. It worked!'

'T'riffic,' panted the old hare. 'Now for the hard part.' So saying, he turned and walked determinedly back into the jungle.

Trundle knew exactly what he meant: Esmeralda still needed a ducking. He didn't envy Ishmael that particular duty!

Jack rose to the surface with an amazed expression on his face. 'Well, I never,' he said, beaming at Trundle. 'So that's what Ishmael feels like most of the time! I must say, I quite enjoyed it – although I can see how it gets in the way of normal life.'

'But did you notice?' said Trundle. 'The pollen has made Ishmael sane.'

'Well, three cheers for that, I say,' said Jack, paddling over to Trundle. 'Life is going to be far easier if he stays that way.'

'Get your paws off me, you jug-headed jackrabbit!' raved a well-known voice. 'Just let me get to my feet and we'll settle this once and for all.'

Ishmael emerged from the trees shortly afterwards, dragging Esmeralda by one foot while she kicked and writhed and fought to get free.

'You'll thank me for this when you're feeling better,' gasped the exhausted hare, hauling her to the bank of the swamp.

'I'll kick your cottontail up the back of your neck, that's what I'll do!' yelled Esmeralda. 'Do you know who you're dealing with, you flop-eared fool? I'm a Roamany princess, I am!'

'Yes,' groaned Ishmael. 'A Roamany princess who's entirely off her pie-crust! Now then – don't make a fuss and this'll all be over before you know it.'

He released Esmeralda's foot and leaned over to try and grab her. But she was too quick for him. She

scrambled to her feet in an instant, her face furious.
But before she could deliver a roundhouse punch to his
snout, he ducked, grabbed her around the waist, and
propelled her to the very brink of the swamp.

She teetered, her feet slipping on the wet grass.
'Nooooooo!' she hooted, losing balance.

'Sorry!' puffed Ishmael, letting go and giving
her a good shove.

At the very last moment, she managed to get a
grip on his shirt-front.

'Whoop!' she exclaimed as she fell.

'Yoop!' he gasped as she dragged him after her.

SPLASH!

For a few seconds the world vanished in a great
fountain of brown swampwater. A wave washed
Trundle to the bank and he clambered out. Jack pulled
himself out a moment or two later and stood shivering
on the bank, wringing his tail out. The swamp was

seething like a cauldron of simmering soup, and bobbing up and down in the swell were the faces of Esmeralda and Ishmael.

'Good gracious me!' said Esmeralda. 'Whatever was I thinking with all that running round and round?' She swam strongly to the bank and Trundle helped her out. 'That dark lotus pollen is tricky stuff, and no mistake,' she said, wiping water out of her eyes. 'What a good thing Ishmael was turned sane! Who knows what would have become of us otherwise!'

'My thinking exactly,' said Jack. 'Three cheers for Ishmael! Hip! Hip! Hoo—'

'Hold on a minute,' Trundle said. 'Why isn't he trying to get out?'

Sure enough, the old hare was making no effort to get to the bank. Instead he was lying on his back, splashing his feet and sending up spouts of water from his mouth.

'Ishmael!' called Jack. 'Are you all right?'

'It's winkles at dawn, Sir Godfrey!' warbled the happy hare. 'Come on in! The custard is lovely!'

There was a telling silence between the three friends.

'Drat!' said Esmeralda. 'Barmy again!' She looked from Jack to Trundle. 'So?' she said. 'Who's volunteering to go in and get him?'

The sun had risen in a bright and warm morning and the four companions were drying out nicely around a merry little campfire, over which fresh-caught fish and green bananas were roasting on a spit.

Esmeralda had laid the fire while Jack had caught the fish and Trundle had found the bananas, making sure to avoid going anywhere near the grove of dark lotus plants. He had seen quite enough of them for one lifetime.

Ishmael, meanwhile, sat happily by the fire, humming contentedly to himself and counting his fingers, toes, ears and whiskers. It seemed to keep him happy, although Trundle thought it was a great shame that his brain had gone to pieces again.

'That was a very strange experience,' said Jack, looking up from a half-eaten fish. 'Do you know, at one point I'd swear I saw a stone windship in the jungle! Isn't that the craziest thing?'

Esmeralda stopped chewing and stared at him, swallowing hard. 'Me, too,' she said. 'A huge stone windship. It looked as if it had gone prow-first into the side of a rocky hill.'

'With full sails and everything,' added Trundle. He pointed away into the trees. 'It was over there somewhere.'

'We can't all have imagined the same thing, surely?' said Jack. He turned to the humming hare. 'Ishmael? Did you see a stone windship earlier on, old chap?'

'Never leave your granny in the rain,' chortled the hare. 'The poor old girl may slither down the drain.'

'I swear he's got worse,' sighed Esmeralda. She turned to the others. 'I'm not so sure that was an imaginary windship at all,' she said. 'What say we go check it out?'

'I'm with you,' said Jack. 'A stone windship in the middle of the jungle. Well, if that isn't a mystery, then I don't know what is. What do you say, Trundle?'

Trundle swallowed a final piece of fish and licked the juices off his fingers. 'What are we waiting for?' he asked, feeling quite adventurous now he knew that no pirates or evil aunties were likely to be involved.

Having kicked out the fire, they gathered up Ishmael and headed off into the jungle. They were very careful to give the dark lotus plants a wide berth – and they also kept a keen eye out for any fearsome beasties or low-flying vampire bats that might have been up and about. Trundle led the way: he had a pretty good idea where he thought he had seen the windship from which the non-existent pirates had come streaming.

He was right! They had not gone very far at all before they saw a huge grey shape through the trees. Pressing on, they pushed lianas and ferns aside with a growing sense of excitement as they approached the curious windship.

At last they found themselves in a clearing among the long-fallen trunks of ancient trees, gazing up spellbound at the huge hulk of a great stone windship. It was of an old-fashioned, highly decorated design that Trundle had only previously seen in history

books; fully rigged, with its sail belling and its powerstone clearly visible between the bars of the mast-top cage. Without the strange and uncanny attributes of powerstone, no windship could fly the skies of the Sundered Lands, but why that particular detail needed to be so exquisitely picked out on a vessel carved from solid stone was anyone's guess.

The windship had obviously been there for some time, as the jungle had moved in on it. Tendrils and creepers laced the tall sides of the hull, threading in and out of the scrollwork rails and festooning the vessel in lush greenery and exotic and colourful blooms. Thriving plant-life could even be seen higher up, twining in leafy green loops around the masts and the rigging.

'It's like a windship from the old days,' Trundle breathed, goggling up at the towering hull. 'The really old days, I mean.'

'I know,' said Jack in awe. 'It's the sculpture of a wind-galleon from the very dawn of time.'

Esmeralda looked at them. 'But who could have carved it?' she asked. 'And how did it get here, in the middle of nowhere?'

Those seemed to Trundle to be very good questions indeed.

5

The Stone Galleon

Something about the massive sculpture of the galleon puzzled Trundle enormously. 'Why did the sculptor carve it with a broken front end?' he asked.

It was a good point, as everyone admitted.

The stone galleon looked as if it had crashed down from the sky, and had been brought to a sudden stop when its prow struck the solid rock wall of a steep hillside. But the damage to the prow wasn't what they would have expected from one stone thing hitting another. There were no lumps and chunks of stone strewn about. In fact, the split stone planks and boards and rails of the bashed-in prow had been carved to resemble broken and splintered timbers.

'It's as if . . .' Esmeralda began hesitantly, 'as if the sculptor *wanted* the galleon to look like it had crashed into the rockface.'

'Except that doesn't make any sense,' said Jack.

'And there's no point putting a statue in the middle of the jungle,' Trundle added. 'No one comes here – it said so in the guide.'

'Why spend months and months on such an amazingly detailed sculpture if no one's going to see it?' Esmeralda agreed.

'I see it!' said Ishmael. He rubbed his bulging eyes and stared up at the galleon. 'Clear as day, it is! Don't you see it?'

'Yes, we all see it,' said Jack. 'That's not the

point. The point is – what's it *doing* here?'

'I don't see it doing anything at all,' said Ishmael.

Trundle pointed up at the buckled prow. 'Is that a name-plate I see up there?'

The crawling tendrils had half-hidden the name, but now they all looked, they were just about able to make it out.

The Gallant Fourth of Six.

'Well, that's an odd thing to call a galleon, I must say,' said Jack. 'I wonder what it means?'

'Who's for going aboard to find out?' asked Esmeralda. She pointed to a stone rope ladder hanging from the galleon's side. 'There might be a plaque or something to tell us who made it and why.'

'Mince me giblets and call me Petunia!' said Ishmael. 'You'll not get me aboard that thing!'

'Then wait here for us like a good loony,' said

Esmeralda. 'We won't be long. Trun? You coming?'

'You bet,' said Trundle, his curiosity well and truly piqued.

Jack went up the stone ladder in no time, but it took the two hedgehogs a good deal of puffing and blowing before they finally made it up to the galleon's rail.

Jack was perched there, his eyes like saucers.

He had good reason to look stunned and amazed.

The deck and rigging of the galleon swarmed with a stone crew; all of them hedgehogs, and most of them carved as though going about their ordinary duties: climbing up the stone rigging, sewing canvas sheets, swabbing decks, polishing the masts and undertaking every other kind of windship endeavour that could be imagined. A few were even gathered around a stone musician playing a stone concertina, carved as though they were singing along.

'They're all wearing very old-fashioned clothes,' Trundle said, stepping gingerly among the bizarre statues. 'I suppose that's so they look right to be on board such an old galleon.' He peered into the face of one of the sailor hedgehog statues. 'Life-sized,' he murmured. 'And so detailed! Every prickle, every whisker . . .' He shook his head. 'It's almost as if . . .'

'As if they aren't statues at all,' finished Esmeralda, walking towards a raised rostrum amidships. She glanced over her shoulder at them. 'I was thinking the same thing. And have you noticed? Some of them look frightened.'

She was right. Although many of the hedgehog sky-sailors had normal expressions, a few looked terrified, and now Trundle looked more closely, some were cowering on the decks with their arms over their faces. A few were even sprawled on the deck as if

they'd been knocked clean off their feet by some
terrific impact.

'Just the way you'd look if you were about to
crash prow-first into a hillside,' commented Jack.
'Is it just me, or is there something very creepy about
all of this?'

'Creepy's the word,' said Esmeralda, climbing
the three steps up to the rostrum. 'Hmmm. There's
something up here you'll want to see.'

Trundle and Jack joined her
on the small rostrum. It
contained a lectern, over
which leaned the statue of
an elderly hedgehog with a
furrowed brow and a quill in
his paw. He had been carved
as though in the middle
of writing in a large open

book. At his feet under the lectern was the carving of a box with its lid open.

'I have a bad feeling about this,' muttered Jack, as the three of them leaned in to see what had been written in the book.

'It's a windship's log,' said Esmeralda, brushing dirt and dead leaves off the stone pages. 'Hmm. Interesting . . .'

They all rose on to tiptoe to read the first entry, way up in the top lefthand corner.

16th of Greengrow

The Spell of Unbinding has unleashed terrible supernatural storms that have caused us to run aground at the wrong end of this benighted rock. We must somehow strive to get our precious cargo up to the snow pinnacle before the midsummer melt is over and the Ice Gate freezes again. That means reaching the Ice Gate by sunset on the 21st of

Greengrow. A daunting endeavour!

'What does it mean?' Trundle asked uneasily.

'The Spell of Unbinding,' murmured Jack. 'Lawks! That was the spell the Badger Lords of Old were attempting when the whole world blew up in their faces.'

Esmeralda nodded solemnly. 'The spell that went horribly wrong and caused the creation of the Sundered Lands – thousands of years ago.'

Trundle's mouth fell open. 'So . . . this sculpture was put here to commemorate the creation of the Sundered Lands?' he ventured.

Esmeralda looked at him. 'Read on,' she said.

17th of Greengrow

Terrible tidings to relate! Originally we thought only a few of our crew had been affected when we crashed. But it has become clear that the magic is leaking from our powerstone into the surrounding rocks and – oh, the horror! – there is a mystical feedback which is turning The Gallant Fourth of Six *and everyone aboard into stone!*

'Not a sculpture at all,' gasped Trundle. 'Real people . . . turned to stone . . . oh, my! Oh, dear! Oh, no, no, no!' He put his paws up over his eyes, not wanting to look into the dreadful stone faces any more.

'Stout heart, Trundle, my lad!' said Jack. 'All this happened thousands of years ago. And that explains the galleon's name: *The Gallant Fourth of Six*. D'you see? This must have been one of the six legendary galleons that carried the Crowns of the Badger Lords to the far-flung corners of their blown-up world. Uncover your eyes, Trundle. Take a look at what was written next.'

18th of Greengrow

I, Ramalama, make this last entry. So few of us are left alive now. I hold the precious Crown of Ice between my mortal hooves! As the Keeper of the Crown, it is for me to make my way alone up to the snowy peaks while the Ice Gate remains open. I have only three days to reach the summit! The Gate of Ice is only melted between the 19th and 21st of Greengrow each year. I go now, leaving only faithful old Buffer Trug here to keep a final record of our doomed voyage. Farewell!

There was only one entry after that – and Trundle could hardly bear to read it.

19 Gr'grow

All is stone now. I can barely lift my arm to write. Must trust that R succeeds. Our only hope now is

And that was it. The stone quill rested still on the stone book, the bent figure of Buffer Trug stooping for ever, staring down with his blind stone eyes on an entry he would never ever finish.

Trundle shuddered from snout to toe.

'My guess is that the Crown of Ice was kept in this box,' said Jack, tapping the stone box under the lectern with his foot. He frowned, scanning the book again. 'There's something strange about the entry made by the Keeper, though.'

'Different writing, that's obvious,' said Esmeralda.

'But that's not all,' said Jack. 'Look. He writes: *I hold the precious Crown of Ice between my mortal hooves!* Do you see? Hooves!'

Trundle wrinkled his brow. 'Hedgehogs don't have hooves,' he said. 'Paws, yes – hooves, definitely not.' His eyes widened. 'So Ramalama, the Keeper of the Crown, wasn't a hedgehog like everyone else here. But what *was* he, then?'

'Plenty of people have hooves,' said Esmeralda. 'My guess he was someone high up in the Badger Lords' court. A horse, maybe? A goat, or a pig, even?

Who knows? Anyway, I think we've seen all we need to see up here. Who's for getting off this horrible galleon before we all die of the terminal creepies?'

'Count me in!' said Jack.

Trundle was as glad as the others to clamber down the stone rope ladder and leave the stone vessel and its forlorn, frozen crew to be slowly engulfed by the jungle. Theirs was a fate that it was altogether too sad even to think about.

But Trundle *was* thinking as he came down to ground level again. He was thinking quite hard.

'Cast off, my merry mates!' said Ishmael. 'Did ye find grollikins and dandoes galore in the scuppers?'

'Not now, Ishmael, if it's all the same to you,' sighed Esmeralda. 'We're feeling a bit gloomy at the moment.'

'It's always darkest before the prawns,' Ishmael said comfortingly.

'And we have learned some useful information about the Crown of Ice,' said Jack. 'It's monstrous sad up there, to be sure, but we ought to look on the bright side of things.'

'I know,' said Esmeralda. 'But I can't help feeling sorry for all those people. I mean, what a ghastly way to go.'

'Excuse me,' Trundle asked. 'What day did we arrive at Tenterwold?' He had cast his mind back to their adventure before last.

'The 12th of Greengrow,' said Esmeralda.

'I thought so.' Trundle did some rapid calculations on his fingers. He looked up, grinning from ear to ear. 'Well, isn't that interesting! By my reckoning that makes today the 21st of Greengrow.'

Jack's eyes lit up. 'And according to the records up there,' he began, 'the Ice Gate melts annually between the 19th and the 21st. Suffering smerks! If

that Ramalama chap fulfilled his task, and hid the
Crown of Ice behind the Ice Gate, we've arrived here
quite by chance on the very last possible day to get up
there and grab it.'

'Quite by *chance*?' hooted Esmeralda. 'Are you
kidding me? This isn't *chance*, Jack, this is the Fates
working flat out in our favour!'

'I rather think it must be,' said Trundle, looking
up into the blue sky. The sun was already climbing up
over the jungle trees and the morning was wearing
away. 'But I wish your dratted Fates had got us here a
day or two sooner. We only have till sunset today to
get to the Ice Gate – then
it'll be frozen again for
another year.'

'So what are we
standing about gabbing
for?' exclaimed

Esmeralda. 'Let's get moving, my lads! Best foot forward, and all that. The last one to the Ice Gate is a prickly poltroon!'

6

Wingnut Flange

It was a hard slog to get through the steamy jungle. Trundle guessed that in more civilized places people would be sitting down for elevenses right about now. But they finally emerged from the trees and felt a fresh, open breeze on their faces.

Ahead of them, the steep-sloping landscape stepped gradually upwards in a series of ridges and ledges, upon which flourished long ranges of small, neatly trimmed bushes. Narrow brown pathways

snaked their way up through these lush green terraces. Dozens of busy workers could be seen, moving slowly and methodically among the bushes, clipping the leaves and putting them into trailing white linen sacks.

They had evidently arrived at the foot of the Lowspace Tea Plantations. Some distance above them, they could now see the wooden platform that they had previously observed from the deck of *The Thief in the Night*. It looked even more extraordinary now, looming out like a jutting roof or a great parasol made of wood, blocking out the view of whatever lay above, and supported all along its curved length by great heavy timbers and massive iron brackets.

'More climbing,' muttered Trundle, eyeing the spiralling and zigzagging pathways that led up to Boardwall, as the guide had told them this amazing structure was called.

'Stout heart, Trundle!' remarked Jack, slapping

him on the back. 'The sooner we get to Downtown, the sooner we can take a breather.'

'Only a quick breather,' Esmeralda warned as she began to plod up the nearest of the serpentine pathways. 'We haven't got all day, you know.'

'I thought we *did* have all day,' Trundle said, following on.

'Yes, to get right up to the top of the island!' Esmeralda called back. 'So no dawdling.'

As the four companions climbed, they could see lines of workers moving up the paths, their linen sacks stuffed with newly clipped leaves. They were all heading for the underside of Boardwall. Once there, Trundle saw that the contents of the sacks were tipped into huge canvas bags, which were then attached to long ropes and winched up through trapdoors and hatches in the underside of the great wooden platform. The growing and harvesting of these bushes was clearly a major industry on Spyre.

'They seem to like their tea, here, don't they?' Jack remarked, unnecessarily.

They continued to climb, waving and calling cheerful greetings to the plantation workers, most of whom waved back and replied along the lines of, 'Nice day for strollings, if not got workings to do!' or 'What happen? You get lost or someone?' and similar friendly comments.

And so they made their winding way up through the plantation as the long hot morning ebbed away.

'A stitch in time is worth two in the bush,' said Ishmael at one point, wiping his sweating brow. 'But even the weariest gibbon winds at last to tea!'

'I'm sure he does,' Trundle said sympathetically. 'But it's not so very far to go now.' In reality he was rather enjoying himself. The climb was steep, but a fresh and sweet-scented breeze cooled his face – and for once nobody was chasing them.

As adventures went, this was the best one so far.

Finally, they came to the upper level of Lowspace, where the ground was dry and full of rocks. At last, they stood directly under the great overhanging shadow of Boardwall, breathing hard and gathering themselves. All around them, plantation workers trudged endlessly up with their laden sacks, and then trudged down again with empty bags to fill them once more. More labourers attached the bulging sacks to dangling chains and ropes, shouting to their co-workers up above, 'From me – to you! Carefully, now! Winch away! Mind your headings! Oops! Sorry about that! Rub it hard and soon better feelings!' Chains clanked and ropes creaked as the full bags were raised up through the trapdoors and empty ones lowered in exchange.

Although the workers seemed quite cheerful,

Trundle had to admit to himself that there was something especially appealing about being a bold adventurer when the alternative was toiling away on a tea plantation!

Esmeralda didn't give them very much time to stand and stare, though. With an imperious wave of her arm, she strode up to the foot of a long ladder that led to a closed hatch high above. Without even looking back to check they were following, she began to climb. Jack went next, his rebec strapped to his back. Ishmael was close behind, and Trundle brought up the rear. The four panting friends were able to gather and catch their breath on a small wooden platform, from which a stair of ten wide wooden steps led up to the closed hatch.

Trundle stepped over to the brink of the platform and looked down. The view was spectacular and breathtaking, the green tea-terraces tumbling away to the distant line of the jungle. But the drop made his head feel giddy and he quickly stepped back from the edge.

'Who wants the honour of being the first to see the wonders of Downtown?' asked Esmeralda, looking hard at him.

'Me, I suppose,' he said resignedly.

'That's my plucky pal!' chuckled Esmeralda. 'One hand on your sword hilt, Trun – just in case.'

'In case of what?'

'Oh, nothing.'

'Hmm.' Trundle made his way up the steps, a paw ready on the hilt of his sword . . . *just in case*. There was a lever on the underside of the hatch. He grabbed it and yanked. The trapdoor sprang open with a speed that took him by surprise.

But what was even more shocking was the sudden noise that came crashing in on his unsuspecting ears. He winced at the appalling racket. It sounded to him like ten thousand people all shouting at the tops of their voices, accompanied by the rumble of wheels and the tramping of feet and the ringing of dozens of gongs and bells.

And while he was still trying to cope with the cacophony, several pairs of thin, furry arms came snaking down through the hatch, grabbing him by every available portion, and lifting him clear off his feet. His eyes boggling, he rose up through the hatch and found himself deposited on a solid plank floor, surrounded by the most extraordinary creatures he had ever seen in his life.

They were meercats – dozens of them, crowding around him, dressed in brightly patterned, short-sleeved shirts and wide-bottomed, baggy shorts. Most of them wore hats – everything from flat caps and bowlers to Stetsons and top hats – and all of these hats had some kind of advertisements printed on them or pinned to them or poking up from the brims.

And all of the meercats were speaking at once.

'Welcome to Downtown, mister pilgrim, sir!'

'Carry your bags, mister?'

'Cheap hotel – very clean!'

'All-day breakfast at the Magnanimous Rissole Restaurant!'

'Monastery tours – suit all pockets!'

All the while, the meercats plucked and pulled at him and fought to get his attention until it all became too much even for such a mild-natured fellow as Trundle.

'Get! Off! Me!' he bellowed, drawing his sword and waving it in the air above his head. The meercats went scooting backwards with startled faces and staring eyes.

Esmeralda emerged from the hatch at his side. 'Well done, Trundle,' she said admiringly. 'That certainly got their attention!' She rested her fists on her hips and surveyed the ring of temporarily silent creatures.

'So?' she said. 'What have we here?'

One of the meercats sidled closer, blinking nervously at them through round wire-framed spectacles. 'He has quick temper, lady!' he said. 'No need for swords. We're only trying to make a living, why not?'

Now that the meercats weren't molesting him and yelling in his ears, Trundle had a few moments to gaze around at Downtown – and the sight quite took his breath away. It was a scene of the most astonishing bustle and clutter and hurrying-scurrying chaos that he had ever witnessed!

There were people everywhere, racing helter-skelter in all directions, some unencumbered, others carrying heavy loads on their backs or drawing laden wagons.

Some of the houses and shops and warehouses had been built out on Boardwall itself, but the teeming city also climbed up the hillside: houses on top of houses, shops and emporia and other buildings crowding in on one another in terraces that were at least as steep as those of Lowspace. Instead of streets, the upper regions of Downtown were reached by wide stone stairways that thronged with people coming and going.

The colours were absolutely dazzling, both in

85

the clothes of the people and in the flags and banners that hung everywhere. There were fiery scarlets and sky blues and luscious greens and sunflower yellows. There was flame orange and turquoise and aquamarine and crimson and mauve. Trundle strained his neck to look up at rainbows of brightly coloured silk pennants that fluttered from rooftops and from doorposts and flagpoles.

Dotted among the close-packed buildings were wooden wharves and jetties, where scores of windships and skyboats were moored. Many of the windships appeared to be permanent fixtures, converted into shops and restaurants and hotels, the hulls and masts festooned with coloured bunting, and with bridges and railed boardwalks leading up to their decks.

Above the chaotic riot of Downtown, Trundle saw the tall white walls and square towers of the lofty monasteries reflecting the bright sunlight, red and yellow banners rippling in the breeze above coral-coloured roofs. And as a final, awe-inspiring sight, there rose far above the monastery the dazzling white peak of the mountain of Spyre. Trundle shivered with wonder and with a strange sensation of apprehension. There was something venerable and dreadful about those snowy slopes, as if they guarded enormous and appalling secrets.

Meanwhile, as Trundle stared speechless, Jack and Ishmael had joined them, and Esmeralda had grabbed the nearest meercat by the collar.

'We need to get to the Ice Gate as quickly as possible, my lad,' she said in her best no-nonsense voice. 'Can you take us there?'

The meercat nodded frantically. 'Sure thing,' he yammered. 'But Ice Gate is expensive tour. Normally ten sunders each. I can do it for seven. Special party rate. Why not? My uncle Flogger works in pilgrim hospitality department.' He blinked from one to the other of them, rubbing his paws together and grinning hopefully. 'Is that good deal?'

'Try five sunders each,' suggested Esmeralda.

The meercat turned to Trundle and winked. 'Your lovely wife – she knows how to haggle, yes?'

Trundle nearly jumped out of his boots at the suggestion that he was married to Esmeralda. 'Excuse me,' he gasped, his face going pale at the very thought. 'We are *not* married!'

At this the meercat grinned wider than ever and gave him a long, slow wink from behind his wire spectacles. 'That's fine, too!' he said. 'None of my business.' He swung around to look at Esmeralda. 'Look, I cut my own throat, but I like you,' he announced. 'Five sunders it is. Come, come – we start tour now. I take you up One Thousand Steps of Radiant Wisdom. You like that!'

'And will that get us to the Ice Gate before sunset?' asked Jack.

'Sure thing, boss. Why not?' replied the grinning meercat. 'I do that for you, no problem.' He patted his chest. 'My name is Wingnut Flange, but you call me Wingnut, why not?'

Trundle and Esmeralda looked at one another.

'Well?' said Trundle. 'Why not, indeed!'

7

Rissoles!

'Making ways, here!' shouted Wingnut, catching hold
of Esmeralda's arm and towing her through the
clamouring crowd of meercats. 'These pilgrims very
much spoken for! Lay off! Party of four coming
through!'

Trundle and Jack darted after them, Jack taking
a firm grip on Ishmael to make sure he stayed with
their party. You never could tell what Ishmael would
do next, and if the old hare went wandering off in this

crush of people, they might never find him again.

Wingnut led them away from Boardwall and up through the narrow, teeming streets of Downtown. Trundle wished they had time to take in the sights as they rushed past an endless array of colourful pilgrim gift stores and restaurants and boarding-houses and tea-shops, not to mention all the stalls and stands that littered the streets, selling every kind of bric-a-brac imaginable.

Wingnut slowed down as they reached the foot of a wide stone stairway that zigzagged its way up through the commotion and confusion of Downtown. Masses of people were trekking up and down the broad staircase, many of them led by meercats bearing a remarkable similarity to Wingnut.

'This is One Thousand Steps of Radiant Wisdom,' he said, coming to a halt under a high wooden arch hung with bells and silken streamers. He raised an eyebrow and held out a paw. 'You pay now, please, and Wingnut guide you good, why not?'

Esmeralda counted out a handful of sunders that instantly vanished into the deep pockets of Wingnut's oversized shorts.

'You fine folk!' he said. 'I give you best tour ever!'

'We're on a bit of a deadline, Wingnut,' said Esmeralda.

'That fine, too!'

'We must make hay while the shoe shines,' added Ishmael. 'Don't put all your legs in one trouser.'

Wingnut blinked at him. 'Oooohh,' he breathed at last. 'That one wise fella!'

Trundle did his best to suppress an explosion of laughter.

'He certainly has a unique perspective on things,' chuckled Jack.

'He's potty,' said Esmeralda. 'Lead on, Wingnut! Sharp's the word.'

The meercat pointed to a skinny side street that led off from the foot of the One Thousand Steps of Radiant Wisdom. 'Before we begin the climb, we partake of nice cup of tea and optional bun,' he grinned, nodding rapidly. 'It is tradition. All pilgrims do it.'

'We can't waste time, you know,' said Esmeralda. 'We need to get right up to the top before sunset.'

'No problem. Plenty time,' insisted Wingnut. 'Very bad luck for pilgrims to travel up steps without first taking tea.' He nodded enthusiastically. 'Missy will fall and break leg, for sure!'

'I suppose we'd better keep to the traditions,' said Trundle.

'I'm sure we can spare a few minutes,' added

Jack. 'After all – how long can it take to drink a
cup of tea?'

'Hard a'port!' declared Ishmael. 'Run out the
buns!'

Wingnut pointed at Ishmael. 'He totally correct.
You my friends – I lead you plenty good, no fooling.'

'Oh, come on then,' Esmeralda said reluctantly.
'Let's get it over with.'

They trailed after Wingnut along the little side
street until they came to a rickety gangplank that led to
a dilapidated old windship. A sign hung over the front
of the gangplank: *The Magnanimous Rissole
Restaurant*.

'Well, look at that,' said Jack. 'It's the place that
was mentioned in the guide. Esmeralda, you had those
free vouchers last. Do you still have them on you?'

'No, they got lost,' Esmeralda said quickly.

'I saw you tuck them away in your bodice,' said

Trundle helpfully. 'I bet they're still there, despite the crash and everything.'

'You have vouchers?' Wingnut said brightly. 'That good news! That mean you can have tea *and* free meal! All in! You lucky people!'

'Oh, well done, Trundle,' growled Esmeralda, handing the vouchers over. 'I was faking it to save us time – now we have to eat as well!'

'Well, *I* didn't know,' said Trundle. 'And anyway, I'm hungry after that long climb. We can easily afford a few minutes for lunch.'

'You'd better be right!'

Wingnut led them up the gangplank and in through a door in the hull of the windship. It was quite dark and stuffy inside, and the place smelled of burned cooking fat. A few dingy tables were scattered around, lit by candles in bottles. There were no other guests and Trundle noticed that the floor could do with a good sweeping.

'This restaurant is run by my cousin Rachette. It very good, yes? Very exclusive. You pick table, I go speak with chef. Tell her you in big hurry.'

The four companions selected the least grubby-looking table and sat down while Wingnut went scuttling off through a pair of swing doors.

'It could be worse,' Trundle said, rubbing a smear off the knife that was set in front of him.

'Could it?' said Esmeralda. 'How?'

They heard voices arguing from beyond the swing doors. One was Wingnut's and the other came from a female, who was giving him a very hard time, by the sound of it.

Shortly, the doors burst open and a plump meercat emerged, wearing a grimy apron and a fierce and fixed expression. She was carrying a tray upon which stood a large teapot and a set of four small round cups. Without speaking, she slammed the tray down on the table, revolved on her heels and stalked back to the kitchens.

Wingnut came trotting over to the table, wringing his hands and smiling. 'Cousin Rachette in a bit of a snit,' he told them. 'She not like being told to hurry up. But it OK – I smooth it all over for you. No problems. Why not?'

The swing doors banged open and Rachette was with them again. This time she smacked a plate down on the table. 'Optional bun!' she declared, and was gone again before anyone could respond.

Trundle stared at the single, wrinkled old roll.

'Hmmm,' said Jack, pouring the tea. 'I think that bun ought to have been put out of its misery some time ago.'

Wingnut glanced towards the kitchen, then leaned forward conspiratorially. 'No need to eat bun,' he whispered. 'Plenty more food coming right up, why not?'

Trundle sipped the tea. It was very hot and rather stewed and tasted like a cross between dandelions and old socks. He saw Wingnut watching him. 'Delicious,' he said diplomatically, putting the cup down. Judging from the expressions on Jack and Esmeralda's faces, they didn't think much of the tea either, but Ishmael gulped it down, smacked his lips and poured himself a second cup.

'Handsomely does, it now,' he said. 'Over the lips and past the gums, watch out gizzard, here it comes!'

'He real big connoisseur,' said Wingnut with awe in his voice. 'Not everyone appreciate Cousin Rachette's tea.'

They became aware of a squeaking rumble coming from the direction of the kitchen. Moments

later, the doors flew open and a large trolley came
rolling towards them on shrieking wheels. It was being
pushed by three meercats in stained overalls. On a huge
plate atop the trolley sat a steaming rissole – fully half a
metre across and at least fifteen centimetres thick.

'Complimentary rissole thanks to voucher!'
explained Wingnut as the four friends goggled at the
vast glistening burger. 'Speciality of the house. Pilgrim
guests must eat it all up for luck! Very bad manners to
leave any.'

Esmeralda glared at Trundle. 'See what you've

landed us with?' she hissed. 'You and your big mouth!'

Trundle stared uneasily at the vast rissole as it was loaded on to their table, taking up most of the surface. He gulped and reached for his knife and fork.

They had some heavy work ahead of them!

'My stomach feels like I've eaten an entire poached walrus, tusks and all,' groaned Jack as the four friends staggered breathlessly up the first few of the One Thousand Steps of Radiant Wisdom, some half an hour later. 'What was that thing made of – old cannonballs?'

'Cousin Rachette she make plenty fine stomach-filler, yes?' said Wingnut, turning back to grin at his four labouring and lagging pilgrims.

'Stomach-filler?' gasped Trundle. 'I feel like I'm full to the eyebrows.'

'Eyebrows nothing,' moaned Esmeralda. 'That stuff is coming out of my ears!'

'Very tasty,' commented Ishmael, picking at his teeth with an extended claw. 'Very sweet. Full of goodness – it went down a treat!'

'What I tell you?' said Wingnut. 'He one big connoisseur of fine food.'

'Just get us up this staircase,' demanded Esmeralda, clutching her midriff. 'And no more distractions.'

'Sure thing, Missy,' said Wingnut, whom Trundle had noticed had not eaten a single mouthful of his cousin's rissole. 'Why not?'

But the trek up the stairway wasn't quite that easy. The stairs were full of people coming and going, as well as masses of touts and hawkers and peddlers trying their best to get Trundle and the others to buy their gifts and souvenirs.

Progress was so slow that eventually Esmeralda lost her rag. She grabbed Wingnut and brought his snout right up to hers. 'Now listen here, Mr Flange,' she snarled. 'It's well past midday. You promised you'd get us all the way up to the top. So snap to it – find us a quicker way up or I'll tie your ears to your feet and use you as a hoop!'

Wingnut stared at her in consternation. 'You don't like cultural artefacts and purchasing opportunities on the way to Radiant Wisdom?' he asked in obvious surprise.

'No, I don't!' Esmeralda yelled.

Wingnut grinned. 'You one feisty lady,' he said. 'I take you on express route. Not usually for pilgrims, but I do special favour for good friends, why not? This way for quick trip to top!'

So saying, he dived off to one side, with Trundle and the others in hot pursuit. He led them through alleys and passageways until they came to a door that bore the legend: *Garden of Serenity*.

'We don't have time for serenity,' said Trundle. 'We just need a quick way up this wretched island!'

'A wretched island is a meal to shake hands with in the dark,' chortled Ishmael.

'So true,' nodded Wingnut. 'Your friend – he clever guy.' He smiled at Trundle. 'Not to worry, mister, sir,' he said. 'This lead to quick way up – and everyone love the Garden of Serenity. It is number one pilgrim spot! You'll see.'

He opened the door and they followed him into a small vestibule with yet another door at the other end. The first door closed behind them with the sharp click of a lock.

'No way back, alas,' Wingnut now confided in them. 'Serenity is one-way trip.'

He opened the door ahead to reveal a small

open courtyard absolutely packed with people, shoulder-to-shoulder. A general hubbub of voices was pierced by the cries of meercat guides, bearing coloured pennants on sticks and yelling instructions.

'You have *got* to be kidding me,' exclaimed Esmeralda, staring at the tightly wedged pilgrims.

'No kiddings,' Wingnut called back as he squeezed into the seething and jostling throng. 'Follow me! Keep close!'

'Garden of Serenity?' groaned Esmeralda as she elbowed her way in among the milling hordes. 'I'll give him Garden of Serenity!'

8

Too Late!

'Oh, sorry!' said Trundle. 'Excuse me!' he added. 'Oh, I do beg your pardon, madam, I thought those were a pair of cushions.' He was trying his very best to be polite as he nudged and edged his way through the multitudes crammed into the Garden of Serenity. But it wasn't easy. As he struggled along in Esmeralda's wake, he would every now and then get an elbow in the ear or a finger up the snout or a faceful of someone's anatomy.

'Blow me!' he heard Jack puffing at his rear. 'They go for rather disorderly serenity around here. Excuse me, sir – that was my tail you just stepped on! Ishmael, keep with me, there's a good fellow.'

'Out of the flying pig and into the liar, as my old mother used to say!' warbled Ishmael in a crushed-sounding voice. 'Steer small, Mister Nibbly! Steer small!'

'Wingnut?' Esmeralda's voice rose above the babble of contesting voices.

'Yes, Missy?'

'I'm going to strangle you when we get out of this!'

'Ha, ha! You one funny lady!'

'That's what *you* think.'

'We almost through now. Not far to go.'

Trundle advanced slowly, pushing and shoving and apologizing, feeling like a hedgehog caught in a

cider press. Then Esmeralda came to a sudden,
unexpected halt and he rammed into the back of
her neck.

'Oww!' he moaned, wishing he had space to lift
an arm to rub his throbbing snout. 'What happened?'

'I'm not sure,' gasped Esmeralda. 'There's a
door. Wingnut is just getting a key . . . and . . .
ahhhh!' Esmeralda lurched forward and Trundle and
the other two went tumbling in her wake.

They had fallen through a narrow doorway and
were sprawled gasping on the floor of a quite small
box-shaped room. Wingnut stepped over them and
closed the door on the Garden of Serenity. Then he
pulled a metal grill across before turning to them,
grinning and nodding.

'This is the way we move things quickly between
bottom and top of stairways,' he explained with a wink.
'One Thousand Steps strictly for pilgrims!'

They disentangled themselves and got to
their feet.

'There's no way out,' Trundle said, frowning at
their guide. 'What's the game?'

He was quite right. Apart from the doorway
through which they had come, the walls of the little
box-room were smooth and featureless, save for an odd
mechanical device set against the far wall, and an eye-
level lever-type thing a little way from it.

'I recognize this,' said Jack,
walking to the machine, which had
ratchets and cogwheels attached
and from which
extended a long
dog-legged
handle. 'It's a
winch!' He turned to
Wingnut. 'We're in some

kind of freight elevator, aren't we?' he said. 'I've seen these things before.'

'That's right!' beamed Wingnut. 'Elevator go up – elevator go down. Pretty smooth. Easy to work.' He pointed to the handle. 'Turn clockwise, we go to top; turn other way, we go to bottom. Why not?' He gestured towards the lever on the wall. 'That pretty good brake. Must be put on once locking device is taken off and while handle is not turned – otherwise unhappy event occurs.'

'So, let's get turning,' said Esmeralda. 'Trundle – you take first go, there's a good chap. Let us know when your arms get tired, and Jack can take over.'

Trundle walked over to the winch and stooped to take a firm grip on the handle.

'You ready?' asked Wingnut.

'Ready,' said Trundle.

Wingnut threw off the restraining bar and Trundle began to turn the handle. Cogwheels and ratchets clanked and clonked as the elevator slowly wobbled upwards.

For a little while, the others stood and watched Trundle as he strained at the handle, then they seemed to get bored with that, and sat around, chatting and listening to Jack as he bowed out a tune in rhythm to Trundle's labours.

'How . . . far . . . is . . . it . . .?' Trundle panted after a while. His shoulders were aching and his fingers were going numb.

'Little way yet,' said Wingnut.

Ishmael came and leaned over the winch, gazing at it in fascination and chuckling to himself. 'Well, I'll go to the foot of our gangplank. Who'd have thought it? My, my, my!'

'Mind your ears!' Trundle warned as the hare

leaned in a little further, but Ishmael was so rapt by the workings of the winch that he didn't hear.

Trundle became alarmed as the long floppy ears came perilously close to the cogwheels. 'Ishmael! Be careful!' he said.

A spinning wheel almost snagged one of the hare's ears.

'Watch out!' Trundle bawled, so distracted by the danger Ishmael was in that he let go of the handle to push the hare back.

The elevator shuddered. There was a grinding noise and the handle began to spin quickly in the opposite direction. Trundle had the sensation of his stomach hitting the roof of his skull as everyone began to yell at once.

'You let go of handle!' shrieked Wingnut. 'I tell you not to! Unhappy event! We go smash bang wallop at bottom of shaft!'

The elevator was hurtling downward and rapidly gathering speed.

'Do something!' hollered Esmeralda.

'The brake!' Trundle yelled as he was thrown off his feet. 'Ishmael! Get the brake!'

'Leave it to me!' The hare leaped at the brake lever and hung from it, his feet clear of the floor. 'Ishmael to the rescue!'

The winch handle was whirring faster and faster now, and the whole lift was shuddering and jarring so that it was impossible for anyone to keep upright.

'Old Ishmael, he knows what to do!' yelled the hare, his feet planted on the wall on either side of the brake as he strained backwards with all his might.

'No!' screamed Wingnut. 'No *pull* – turn brake sideways!'

Too late! Ishmael gave a final wrench at the brake . . . and it snapped off close to the wall. He lay on his back with his legs in the air, clutching the brake. 'I got it!' he crowed. 'Ishmael got the brake!'

'He broke the brake!' howled Jack. 'We're doomed!'

'No!' gasped Trundle, getting to his knees and managing to draw his sword. 'I'll jam this in the works. That'll stop us!'

'Don't!' shrieked Esmeralda. 'That sword is part of the prophecy. You can't risk breaking it!'

Trundle stared at her. 'But we'll break every bone in our bodies otherwise!' he shouted.

'Try this!' Jack crawled across the shuddering floor. With a stricken look, he lifted his rebec in his arms and brought it plunging down into the rapidly rotating cogwheels of the howling winch mechanism.

Trundle watched in desperate hope as the machine chewed its way through Jack's rebec. Splinters of wood flew, and there came the sound of snapping strings as poor Jack fed his prized instrument into the whirring winch.

But it was working! Gradually the cogwheels and ratchets slowed. Smoke poured out and, with a smell of scorching wood, the mechanism ground to a standstill and the elevator room stopped shaking and jolting. Trundle felt a firm bump from beneath as the room came to a final halt.

Wingnut staggered to his feet. 'That plenty big piece of luck, there,' he gasped. 'Mister Jack is big hero! Save all our lives.'

Tottering to the metal grill, he dragged it aside and opened the door.

All the overwhelming cacophony of Downtown greeted their ears.

'Well, what you know!' said Wingnut. 'We all the way down to Boardwall again.' He grinned around at them as they started to get up. 'Don't worry,' he said brightly. 'I make no extra charge for two trips up! Hey, Missy! What for you pick up that brake handle? What for you come at me with big scowl on your face? Help! Wingnut want danger money now!'

The afternoon light was failing fast as the flushed party of pilgrims came at long last to the very top of the One Thousand Steps of Radiant Wisdom. It had taken them almost the whole afternoon to struggle up through the masses of people, doing their utmost to move quickly and refusing all offers of souvenirs and gifts on the way.

The walls of the monastery rose majestically above them, glowing golden in the light of the fading sun. A path wound up, leading to a white gatehouse hung with red and yellow flags. Its double doors stood wide open, revealing courtyards and buildings within.

'Made it!' panted Esmeralda, glowering at a

rather nervous-looking Wingnut. 'Now – get us inside there before the sun disappears!'

Almost before the words had left her mouth, the thunderous reverberations of a mighty gong broke the calm of the early evening.

Glonggg! Glongggg! Glo-o-o-ongggggg!

'What's that for?' Trundle asked, his paws over his ears.

'Uh-oh!' said Jack. 'Trouble!'

Even while the deep voice of the gong was still fading, the gates of the monastery swung slowly closed. There was a boom as the doors met. There were the thuds of bolts being thrown across. There was the clank of a key being turned.

'Oh, hard luck!' exclaimed Wingnut. 'Monastery closed for the night.' He shook his head. 'Most unfortunate. You took too long eating that rissole! I thought so at the time.'

Jack and Esmeralda and Trundle turned on him, their expressions ferocious.

'It no big problem!' said Wingnut, backing quickly away. 'My cousin Threejob runs Rest House of Harvest Prune. He take you in. I can arrange special family rates for you fine people.' He grinned hopefully. 'Or maybe I arrange you not pay at all,' he gabbled. 'Why not?'

It was a gloomy party that sat on the balcony of their complimentary sleeping quarters, soaking their aching feet in bowls of warm tea and gazing wistfully up at the mountain. It looked really rather spectacular in the starry night, its upper slopes shrouded in white mist, its high peak lost in a veil of cloud.

'I can't believe we missed the deadline,' groaned Trundle for maybe the fifteenth time. 'And we were so close!'

'And now the Ice Gate will freeze over again,' added Esmeralda. 'And it'll be a whole year till we can get to the Crown of Ice.'

This was a most depressing and miserable end to their adventure. Avoiding the pursuing pirates and Esmeralda's wicked aunty for a few days or weeks was all very well – but for *twelve entire months*? It simply wasn't possible. And if they were unable to lay hands on the Crown of Ice, the prophecy would never be fulfilled and all their efforts so far would have been in vain.

Trundle had the feeling that Jack was the unhappiest of them all. He had sacrificed his beloved rebec and now he couldn't even play them a tune to lighten their mood. Trundle looked at the usually merry minstrel. Jack hadn't spoken for some time. He must be feeling awful. But then Trundle noticed that the squirrel was busy scribbling things down on a scrap of paper resting on his knees.

'What are you doing, Jack?' he asked. 'Writing
a sad song about what happened? A requiem for a
wrecked rebec?'

'Not in the least!' said Jack, his eyes
unexpectedly bright. 'I've been doing some
calculations.' He sat upright and bawled at the top
of his voice. 'Wingnut! Hey, Wingnut – get yourself
in here!'

A few moments later, Wingnut arrived, clad in a
floor-length nightgown and with a nightcap over his
ears, the bobble of which kept swinging to and fro
across his face, making him go cross-eyed behind his
spectacles.

'Yes, Mister Jack, sir?' he said uneasily. 'Is
there more things I can be doings for you? You
peckish? Need snackings? Wish for Wingnut to plump
your pillows? Name it and I do it. I feel disappointings

is maybe my fault.'

'Cheer up,' said Jack. 'You might be able to make everything all right again if you give me the correct answer to one simple question.'

'Ask question, I give good answer, why not?'

'What is the date today?' asked Jack.

'Today is 20th of Greengrow,' Wingnut replied. 'That well easy question! Ask another!'

Esmeralda sat bolt upright, staring at Trundle. 'You prize idiot!' she hollered. 'You said today was the 21st. You worked it out all wrong!'

'We still have a full day to get to the Ice Gate,' added Jack.

'Well, I'll be blowed!' gasped Trundle, not minding in the least being called an idiot under the circumstances. 'So I did! Well, that's the best news I've had for a long time.'

'Toffee makes the donkey's ears sticky when he sees the fishing rod!' added Ishmael, nodding enthusiastically.

'Wingnut very happy for you!' grinned their guide. 'I take you into monastery first thing in morning!'

'No delays,' warned Esmeralda. 'No detours. And definitely no rissoles!'

'Meercats' honour!' said Wingnut, holding up a solemn paw. 'You see Ice Gate in morning. That's a promise. Why not?'

The Ice Gate

The party of five were ready and waiting the following morning when the gongs rang out and the trumpets blared and the great gates of the monastery swung open to greet the new day.

'Follow me!' declared Wingnut, marching in under the high arch of the gatehouse. 'I show you points of interest, why not?'

'Do it quickly,' said Esmeralda. 'Remember what I told you!'

Wingnut nodded very fast. 'Yes, I remember. But this very, very historical place. The First Master – he built it long times ago – most venerable Master Ramalama.'

'Ramalama?' said Jack. 'Well, I never! The brave chap did make it up here after all!'

'Good for Ramalama!' Esmeralda added with a low whistle.

'So the crown ought to be up beyond the Ice Gate still,' said Trundle. 'And the Ice Gate is melted right now. All we have to do is go up and get it!'

Wingnut was looking from face to face as they spoke. 'I take you to Ice Gate in very soon time,' he said. 'But what crown you mean? I can get you crown – very cheap!'

'Not the one we're looking for, you can't,' Esmeralda said, patting him on the back. 'Don't worry about it. Just get us up there.'

Wingnut blinked at her a few times, then turned and went trotting off through the archway and into the grounds of the monastery.

It was clear right from the start that they were in a special kind of place. Trundle could feel the peacefulness of the monastery enveloping him, as though the very walls dreamed tranquil dreams.

'This is the Scarlet Gate of Inquiry,' Wingnut informed them in a low, reverent voice as they passed a carved, arched doorway to one side. They came next into a wide green courtyard. 'And this the Reflective Cloister. Hush – very quiet place where Lamas come to ponder on deep stuff, why not?'

And there, at last, they got their first sight of the legendary Lamas of Spyre. They were actual llamas, all of them dressed in heavy satin robes of midnight blue, and most of them wearing tall curved hats on their heads. They sat or walked slowly about the

cloisters, their heads bowed in thought, their faces wise
and dignified and benevolent.

The four pilgrims followed their guide on
tiptoe, not wishing to disturb the pious creatures.
Wingnut led them on through baileys and courts and
open pathways, across lawns and through blooming
gardens and under white arches, up
stairways and passageways.

And all about them, the serene
llamas sat or stood or paced the
flagstones, all silent, all very
obviously thinking profound
thoughts.

'This very interesting,'
Wingnut explained, stopping
under the shadow of a long
white wall. 'This is the
Seat of the Absent Oracle.'

He pointed to a niche cut in the wall. It contained a simple stone chair with a purple cushion on it. Trundle could see at a glance that the threadbare cushion had been there for some time.

'He's been absent a very long time, that Oracle,' nodded Wingnut. 'About time he turn up again!' He looked at them. 'By the way,' he said. 'I forgot to say – this special tour includes free fortune-telling from mysterious and ancient Badger Blocks. You ever hear of Badger Blocks? They very special – only Lamas can interpret their prophecies.'

'We know all about Badger Blocks, thanks,' said Esmeralda. 'And, trust me, it isn't only these fellows who know how to use them!' She eyed him keenly. 'Now then – what about the Ice Gate?'

'That next stop, Missy,' Wingnut said brightly. 'One long staircase, and we're right there!'

'Where there's a will, there's an anchovy,'

declared Ishmael. 'Cast off, my hearty – Ishmael's a willing!'

Wingnut gazed admiringly at the old hare for a moment, then set off again.

The path to the Ice Gate turned out to be a very long staircase indeed. It wound up the mountainside, climbing over walls and around towers and up steep slopes until pretty much the whole of the extensive monastery complex was spread out below them. As they climbed, Trundle noticed that the air was becoming gradually chillier and chillier. He tucked his paws into his pockets and hunched his shoulders. They were getting closer to the snow.

'There you will see Emerald Prophecy Courtyard,' Wingnut said, turning and pointing back down to the lower parts of the sprawling monastery. 'They working on your fortune-telling right now!'

They looked down. Sure enough, in a wide courtyard striped by mown grass, they saw a whole group of llamas dressed up in four-sided oblong costumes with pictures painted on each side. They were obviously playing the parts of living Badger Blocks!

As they watched, a gong rang out and the Badger Block llamas suddenly took off in all directions. They raced around and around the courtyard, darting this way and that until Trundle felt quite dizzy from watching them. Then a new llama in ultramarine Lama robes strode out, wielding a hooked stick.

He moved among the racing animals, swiping randomly at their feet. Most leaped over the stick, but every now and then one was tripped up and went rolling over and over in the grass. When four llamas had been brought down, the gong sounded again and the rest ran to the sides of the courtyard, while the Lama with the stick walked around the fallen players, writing something down on a scroll.

'Amazing,' breathed Esmeralda. 'What a brilliant way to do a reading.'

'Time to go,' said Wingnut, hopping from foot to foot and blowing into his hands. 'It too nippy for long hangings about!'

Up they went. And then up some more. It wasn't long before Trundle could see his breath as they climbed. There was a powdering of snow on the steps now, and the air nipped with icy teeth at ears and tails and fingers and toes.

But at last they came to the top.

'This is Enlightenment Platform of the Astonishing Ice Gate!' announced Wingnut, stepping out on to a large wooden platform that jutted on solid wooden posts above the lower snow-slopes. The white mountain fairly filled the sky now – huge and strange and enigmatic, wreathed in mists and with its head in cloud.

'Harpoons and hosepipes!' exclaimed Ishmael, staring up at the mountain. 'You may fire when ready, Mr Goosepaste! My endives are at your command!'

'What a brain this man got!' marvelled Wingnut, rubbing his paws together and gazing spellbound at Ishmael. Then he sighed and padded over to a large brass telescope set atop a post in the middle of the platform. 'From here you can see Ice Gate really good,' he said. 'Who wants first lookings?'

'You mean, this is it?' asked Esmeralda. 'You're not going to take us right up to the Ice Gate itself?'

Wingnut's eyes bulged. 'Not jolly likely!' he exclaimed. 'Very dangerous to go any higher. All snow from here on up. No paths. Just plenty big snow snakes that eat you in one gulp.' He flapped his arms, shivering with the cold. 'But you can see the Ice Gate fine from here, no problem.'

'We don't want to *look* at it,' said Jack. 'We want to go *through* it!'

'*Noooo!*' Wingnut stared at them in astonishment. 'You making big joke on Wingnut. No one goes through Ice Gate.' He spread his arms to their fullest extent. 'Snakes, I tell you! Big snakes, no fooling! You don't want to be eaten! Not much fun, trust me!'

'We've handled worse than *snakes*,' Esmeralda said nonchalantly.

'All the same, we ought to take a look at them,' Trundle said uncertainly as he marched over to the telescope. If the snow snakes were as big as Wingnut was suggesting, then they'd need a plan of attack.

The telescope was fixed in position, and the

moment Trundle looked through it, the Ice Gate leaped up to his eye, so huge and clear and shiny that it quite took him by surprise. The telescope was aimed at a deep, narrow ravine cut into the mountainside. Its sides reared up sharp and hard, capped with snow and hung with massive icicles. Trundle couldn't see where the ravine led; a thick mist coiled between the walls, obscuring the view. But it was easy to spot the remnants of the Ice Gate itself. Fragments of it remained, melted to little nubs and stalagmites of clear ice between the lower jaws of the ravine. And it was so close!

Trundle removed his eye from the telescope and suddenly the Ice Gate wasn't close at all. It was a fair way off, in fact, a good trek up the smooth sheer face of the snow-clad mountain.

He looked at the others. 'Anyone got any bright ideas?' he asked.

'We nip over the side of this platform and get

ourselves up there, pronto,' suggested Esmeralda. 'It's not so very far, and even if there are any giant snakes about, surely we can outwit a bunch of overgrown worms!'

Just then, a series of high trumpet calls sounded from the monastery below.

'That's well odd,' said Wingnut, running to the top of the stairs. 'That's the alarm call! Something up!' He stared down, his breath clouding and his arms wrapped around himself for warmth. 'Ah, I see signal flags now.'

Trundle came and looked over his shoulder. Way down in the Emerald Prophecy Courtyard, llamas were waving a series of red and yellow pennants in a way that he assumed must mean something.

Wingnut translated the signals slowly aloud. 'Party . . . of . . . four . . . travelling . . . with . . . guide . . . Wingnut . . . Flange . . .' He broke off, clearly startled. 'Hey, that's me! What I done wrong?'

'Tell us the rest of it,' said Esmeralda, standing now at his side.

'Too right I will, Missy!' declared Wingnut, peering down. 'It say . . . Party of four travelling with guide Wingnut Flange . . . to be nabbed and taken to High Lama without delay. Have a nice day. End of message.' He turned to them, his eyes like saucers. 'Who are you?' he said crossly. 'I never been in trouble with High Lama before. You bad news, and after all I do for you!'

'I think I know what's happened,' said Esmeralda. 'It's that darned free Badger Block prophecy. It's told them what we're here for – and I don't think they like it!'

'And here they come,' said Jack. 'Dozens of them!'

He was right. Even as they stared down, they

saw a whole posse of Lamas streaming up the stairs towards them, their robes billowing as they ran.

'Oh, excellent,' groaned Esmeralda. 'All this way only to be thwarted by a bunch of monks.'

'Not if we run for it!' said Trundle. 'We still have time to escape if we jump off the platform and head up the mountain.'

'Yes, you're right!' cried Jack. 'Especially if they're afraid of the snakes. Sword out, Trundle! Let's go.'

Jack ran for the far side of the platform. For a second, Trundle saw his leaping shape silhouetted against the snow, and then he was gone. Grabbing Ishmael, Trundle followed, Esmeralda close behind.

A catch of the breath, a moment's hesitation on the brink of the platform, and then Trundle was in the air and the snow-banks of the mountain were rushing up to meet him. He plunged up to his knees in crisp, crunchy snow. Jack was already ahead of him, floundering upwards, leaving a deep trough in his wake.

'Ha!' whooped Esmeralda. 'That's outfoxed 'em! Come on, Trun – we're almost there!'

The four of them waded up the mountain, keeping close together and helping one another out when the drifts got especially deep. Trundle could hear shouting from the platform, but he didn't waste any time looking around. His sword was out and ready and he was determined to get to the Ice Gate, no matter what. They were halfway to the ravine already; one last effort and they would be up there, despite the cold and the wet and the hard battle through deep snow.

'Nothing can stop us now,' panted Esmeralda. 'Crown of Ice, here we come!'

Trundle felt a curious rumbling under his feet. Then he saw a long bulge lifting itself up in the snow, running quickly in their direction, as if something huge was tunnelling towards them under the surface.

With startling suddenness, the snow ahead of them erupted, knocking them all off their feet. A frightful spiky, horny head emerged on the end of a long sinuous white-pelted neck. Yellow eyes gleamed and wide red jaws opened. A cruel and icy voice boomed out.

'Aha!' roared the giant snow snake. 'Luncheon!'

10

The Quivering Hoof

'Get behind me!' Trundle yelled to the others as he advanced bravely on the towering monster with his sword at the ready. 'Listen up, snake!' he hollered, his knees knocking as he stared up at the hideous creature. 'I think you ought to know we're on a special quest, and that we've got the Fates on our side. So maybe you'd like to think twice about trying to eat us!'

'Thanks for the warning,' roared the gigantic snow snake. 'But I think I'll scoff you down anyway, if it's all the same to you!'

'Big mistake, snake!' hollered Esmeralda. 'Go get him, Trundle!'

'Poke him in the eye!' yelled Jack, swinging his fists.

'Curse his cutlets!' shouted Ishmael. 'Auctions shriek louder than birds!'

Trundle glanced unhappily at them. His only real hope had been to bluff the snake into leaving them alone. The looming great thing must be fifteen metres long! *Lawks!* Its teeth were almost as long as Trundle's sword! He let out a yelp as the huge head of the monster came hurtling down towards him, jaws wide and eyes blazing.

At the same moment, half a dozen more snow snakes appeared on the scene, their ferocious heads shooting up from the snowfields all around them, their roars making the air shiver. Any one of them was big

enough to swallow the four friends whole. They were utterly surrounded and really rather doomed.

Trundle winced as the snow snake's head descended, its jaws gaping. He braced himself, holding the sword above his head in both hands. Closing his eyes, he offered a quick prayer to the Fates, wondering bleakly what life would be like inside the stomach of a gigantic snake.

But then something quite extraordinary happened.

Through the roaring of the snow snakes, he heard a series of high-pitched whoops and calls that seemed to be coming from further down the mountain. And then, just a few seconds later, there were whizzing and thudding noises all around him and he was suddenly surrounded by flying figures and yelling voices.

He stared around in disbelief.

It was the llama Lamas coming to their rescue! Trundle had never seen anything like it! They came leaping and bounding through the snow like rubber balls, springing up to plant a hoof on a snow snake's snout, then bouncing off, turning somersaults in the air, ready and eager to launch an attack on the next one. Most were unarmed, but a few carried long quarterstaffs that they spun and whirled expertly in their hooves.

'Weeeyaaah!' yelled one llama, landing lightly on the head of the snow snake threatening Trundle. He crouched and raised one hoof above his head. 'Bungi! Bungi!' the llama shrieked, bringing his hoof down between the snow snake's eyes.

The stricken snake toppled forward so abruptly that Trundle had to leap aside so as not to get squashed underneath.

The llama jumped on high, performing a nifty head-over-heels in midair and coming down on one knee right in front of Trundle. He gave a dashing grin as he rose to his feet.

'That was Crouching Tiger to Leaping Mantis,' he said, bowing to Trundle. 'Text-book example of Professor Yip's Third Stratagem!'

'Oh! Really?' Trundle gasped. 'I thought you were thinkers, not fighters.'

'We're both!' exclaimed the Lama. 'Philosophy and punch-ups. Good for mind and body!'

The fight was going very well for the monks. Trundle could see that the bewildered snow snakes were getting a severe beating. Esmeralda and Jack cheered the leaping llamas on as one by one the snow snakes were brought down or sent packing, slithering off up the mountain, weeping and wailing and dragging their bruised tails behind them. Ishmael was turning cartwheels in the snow, cheering at the top of his cracked old voice.

'Ow!' groaned a loud voice. Trundle's snow snake opened an angry eye. 'That hurt!' it roared. 'You'll pay for that, you meddling monk!'

The llama spun around, extending one foreleg towards the slowly rising snake.

'Be gone, foul fiend,' warned the llama. 'Flee while you still can, else I will apply the deadly force of the Quivering Hoof!'

The snake glared down at him for a few moments, as though considering its options. Then, with a mighty snort of rage, it turned and sped off up the

146

mountain, sending up great sheets of snow in its wake.

'The Quivering Hoof, eh?' chortled Esmeralda, helping to dig Trundle out of the avalanche the departing snake had set off. 'I'd like to learn that one.'

'A difficult technique to master without *hooves*,' remarked the llama. He eyed Esmeralda and Trundle sternly. 'But now to more serious matters.'

Now the last of the snakes had been dispatched, the rest of the llamas formed a circle, herding Ishmael and Jack in to stand alongside Trundle and Esmeralda. They folded their fore-hooves into the long sleeves of their robes and stood looking at the four adventurers with grave and solemn expressions on their long faces.

'We're in trouble with the High Lama, then?' said Esmeralda.

'Trouble?' said the first llama. 'Not at all! He wishes to speak with you and share with you the findings of the Badger Block reading.'

'You mean about the crown?' asked Trundle. 'We can explain that.'

The Lama shook his head. 'The Badger Blocks have foretold that one of your number is the Absent Oracle, for whom we have waited time out of mind!'

'Is that a fact?' said Esmeralda, sounding surprised and relieved. 'Well, I'm a Roamany princess,' she continued. 'I know how to use the Badger Blocks and I can do magic and stuff. So I imagine I must be the Absent Oracle you've all been waiting for.' She lifted a wary eyebrow. 'Um . . . is that a *good* thing to be?'

'It is a most wonderful thing to be,' declared the llama.

'Good, then,' said Esmeralda. 'And as I'm this Absent Oracle of yours, I imagine you won't mind me and my pals borrowing the Crown of Ice.' She pointed up to the ravine. 'I take it we'll find it up there?'

'The Crown of Ice is a most sacred artefact,' said the llama. 'The Blessed Ramalama himself placed it there for safekeeping.'

'Yes, we know,' said Jack. 'But we're on a bit of a quest, you see – and we really need that crown.'

'Wait a moment!' said the llama. He beckoned to his companions and the whole group of them went into a huddle together.

'Er, where's Ishmael going?' asked Trundle. While the llamas were busy conferring, the old hare had gone skipping up through the snow, heading for the ravine.

'Get after him!' yelled Esmeralda. 'Who knows what he's capable of doing?'

They chased after him, snow flying as they went.

Ishmael made it all the way to the mouth of the ravine before Jack finally got close enough to grab him. But his cold fingers couldn't do more than catch Ishmael's foot for a moment, tripping the hare so he went bowling off through the melted Ice Gate, all arms and legs and revolving ears. There was a thud and a crack. Ishmael sat up, rubbing his head and looking even less with-it than usual.

The others ran up to him.

'I'm so sorry,' said Jack. 'Did you bang your head?'

'Unhand me, sir! I know the smell of chickens when I see it.'

They helped the woozy hare to his feet. Then Trundle noticed what Ishmael had hit his head on. It was a low pillar of ice set in the very middle of the ravine – and the impact had cracked it open from top to bottom.

'Look what he found!' gasped Trundle, pulling chunks of ice away.

The pillar of ice was quite hollow. Seated on a small stone plinth within it was the lovely and elegant Crown of Ice. And carved into the stone plinth were the words:

I, Ramalama, put this here till the coming of the Absent Oracle. Why not?

Esmeralda reached in and picked up the crown. 'Ooh!' she said. 'Chilly!'

At that moment, the llamas arrived in the ravine. They took one look at the inscription and then, before Trundle knew what was happening, all four of the adventurers were lifted shoulder high by the cheering creatures and carried in

triumph down through the snow and back to the monastery.

Trundle and the others were borne all the way to the throne room of the High Lama. It was a magnificent chamber with soaring white walls and high, arched windows and with cascading banners of yellow and red silk. The High Lama sat in front of them on his jewelled throne. He was an elderly fellow with kindly eyes and a long straggly white beard. Jubilant monks crowded around them, chanting a greeting song for the return of the Absent Oracle. It really was a major celebration!

Esmeralda stood in the centre, somewhat tongue-tied at all the attention, but looking quite pleased with herself at the same time. It took her and the others a little while to explain to the High Lama the reason why they wanted the crown. He listened with a benevolent expression on his friendly old face as they told him about pirates and wicked aunts and the difficulties they had encountered with thirsty vampire bats.

'The Fates would not have brought you here if they had not intended for you to win the Crown of Ice,' the High Lama announced, once they had finished their tale.

'So, you don't mind us taking it away?' Trundle asked.

'The words of The Blessed Ramalama are quite clear,' said the High Lama, leaning down from his lofty throne. 'The Oracle has returned and you may take the crown with you. And to make your journey easier, I will dispatch a few of my monks down to the jungles to retrieve your skyboat and to repair it and to fill it with new provisions.'

'Excellent!' said Esmeralda. 'And as soon as

that's done, we'll be off, if you don't mind.'

The High Lama lifted a hoof. 'Only three of you may depart with the crown,' he announced. 'The Absent Oracle must stay for ever within the precincts of the monastery.'

'Oh,' gasped Esmeralda, going pale. 'I'm not so sure about that . . .'

'It is foretold thus,' said the High Lama. 'But fear not, Esmeralda Lightfoot, your companion will be treated most reverently when he sits upon his glorious cushion.'

'That's all very well, but . . .' She paused, looking puzzled. 'My companion? What do you mean – my *companion*? I'm the Oracle, aren't I?'

'It is another,' said the High Lama.

Trundle had a sinking feeling. If awkward things were going to happen, they generally happened to him. Kind as the monks were, and much as he

admired their monastery, he didn't much fancy
spending the rest of his life sitting on that little
stone seat, cushion or no cushion.

'So, who *is* the Oracle?' asked Jack.

'The Absent Oracle is this worthy hare,'
announced the High Lama.

'Strike me puce and pepper me with
pomegranates!' exclaimed Ishmael, his ears spinning.
'Who'd a thought it?'

For the next few hours, the monastery was a whirl of
activity. Ishmael was whisked away while Trundle and
Esmeralda and Jack were fed and given long hot baths
and generally very well looked after. At first,
Esmeralda was a bit miffed not to have been the
Absent Oracle after all, but she quickly rallied around
and saw the bright side of things.

The Ceremony of the Inauguration of the

Absent Oracle took place at dusk that evening, but in the meantime, several rather encouraging things happened. *The Thief in the Night* was rescued – and the Crown of Fire was still there in its biscuit tin under the stern seat. Artisans and carpenters scurried all over the wrecked vessel, and by the time they had finished, the trim little craft was looking better than ever; in place of its lost sails, they were given sails of purple silk, which looked very splendid indeed.

And as if that wasn't enough to have the three friends cheering from the rafters, the llamas presented Jack with a wonderful new rebec and bow. Of course, he thanked them by writing a quick paean of praise to their kindness and perspicacity, which seemed to go down very well.

At last the time for Ishmael's inauguration arrived. Scores of monks lined the route to the wall where the seat of the Absent Oracle waited. Wingnut stood with Trundle and the others as they waited for the Absent Oracle to appear. Their ex-guide was in good form, grinning from ear to ear and with the pockets of his shorts bulging with gifts given to him by the monks as a reward for his part in the return of the Oracle.

'It just as my cousin Threejob always say!' he chortled cheerfully. 'Good deeds are their own reward, but getting a reward for good deeds is better still. Why not?'

'I couldn't agree more,' said Esmeralda. 'Ah, here he comes. Gosh – just look at our Ishmael! Isn't he a sight for sore eyes?'

The old hare came pacing along between two rows of Lamas, his skinny body lost under billowing purple robes, his ears squished down by a high purple hat. To the call of trumpets and the beating of gongs, Ishmael March, the Absent Oracle of Spyre, took his seat.

A hush came down over the crowd.

'Thus is the bottom of the Perpetual Oracle placed upon the Cushion of Prophecy!' cried the High Lama. 'Oh wise and foresighted Oracle, speak that we shall be enlightened!'

'Radishes, rascals and clocks always come in threes,' declared Ishmael.

'Oh, heck,' mumbled Esmeralda, putting a paw over her eyes.

But the effect on the Lamas was quite extraordinary. Muttering together, they gathered in groups all along the wall, obviously debating the meaning of Ishmael's comment.

'Well, if they go for that kind of thing,' Jack said with a grin, 'old Ishmael should keep them happy for years to come!'

'Absolutely,' agreed Esmeralda. 'And I think it's about time we were off. The Crown of Fire is stowed away safe and sound. And the Lamas have given us a special box to keep the Crown of Ice in so it won't melt.' She patted Wingnut on the back. 'You've been a good pal, Wingnut,' she said. 'We couldn't have managed it without you.'

'No problems, Missy!' Wingnut grinned. 'I get free meals for long time with tales I can tell. Why not?'

'I hate to break the mood,' said Trundle. 'But did anyone notice there wasn't a *clue* with the Crown of Ice?' He looked enquiringly from Jack to Esmeralda. 'I mean to say – where do we go next?'

'Spoons to the left of me, spoons to the right, onward into the rhubarb tart!' said a familiar voice. While the Lamas were pondering his recent pronouncement, Ishmael had left his seat and come up behind the three friends, smiling widely and seemingly delighted with his new office.

'Hello, Mr Oracle,' said Esmeralda. 'I don't suppose you have any words of wisdom that will tell us where to look for the Crown of Wood?'

Ishmael's smile widened. 'This vision has been sent to me, courtesy of the Seat of the Perpetual Oracle,' he said, his eyes glazing over. 'You must travel to the distant and sinister island of Hammerland and seek for the Crown of Wood among the steammoles.'

They gaped at him. 'That actually sounded halfway sensible,' gasped Jack. 'Ishmael? Are you sure about this? Hammerland? The steammoles?'

'Cauliflower cheese, cauliflower cheese!' warbled the hare. 'It's good for your nose and it's good for your knees!' And so saying, he turned and went prancing back to his little seat.

'Do you know where Hammerland is?' Trundle asked his friends.

'Oh, I know where it is, all right,' Jack said darkly. 'That's not the problem.'

'So, what *is* the problem?' asked Esmeralda.

'The steammoles are the problem,' said Jack. 'They don't like visitors to their homeland, not at all they don't.' He rubbed his snout. 'But they aren't the only obstacle,' he added. 'Between here and Hammerland lie the Sargasso Skies – and no one has ever found a way through that foul and rotting mire.'

Well, then,' said Esmeralda, tucking one arm into Trundle's and one arm into Jack's, 'I'd say we've got our work cut out for us!' She gave a carefree laugh. 'Come along, you two! Last one aboard *The Thief in the Night* is a parboiled pilchard!'

And with that, she towed the two of them off to their spirited little skyboat and to further adventures through the vast Sundered Lands!

ALLAN FREWIN JONES
AND GARY CHALK

Allan was born under the kitchen floor of a derelict house in south-east London. At the age of nine, he inherited a typewriter and, for want of anything better to do, began to write stories. He had his first book published at the age of one hundred and three; lots more followed. He has a German wife, an English cat and a collection of old Beano annuals and lives in the same derelict house where he grew up.

Gary was born under a bush and brought up by a family of weasels. He was hopeless in school except for art, English and history, in which he weaselly came top of the class. After working as a teacher for a while, he became an illustrator, and drew the pictures for many of the Redwall books. He lives with his wife in a farmhouse in the French countryside, working in a huge attic.

Read on for the thrilling continuation in:

Sargasso Skies

'Oh, great, Trundle!' groaned Esmeralda. 'Nice going. Now we're stuck!'

Trundle was on the narrow seat in the stern of the skyboat, red-faced and puffing with exertion as he tried to reverse the treadles that worked the propeller. 'How is this *my* fault?' he gasped. 'We were blown in here by a cyclone!' The wooden treadles were locked solid. He peered over the back of *The Thief in the Night*. Their little skyboat hung at an alarming angle, caught up high in the rigging of a wrecked windship. A length of thick, tarred rope had wound itself tight around the propeller blades.

'It *isn't* your fault,' said Esmeralda. 'But I have to blame someone and you're nearest.'

'Many's the windship has foundered in this dreadful gyre,' Jack said, struggling to untangle himself from more rigging that had snagged over the prow. 'I told you we might have problems getting safely past the Sargasso Skies.' He pulled himself loose at last. 'It's the graveyard of countless brave sky-faring vessels,' he said mournfully. 'Why, I could sing you sad ballads of lost and missing windships that would make you weep!'

'Later, maybe,' said Esmeralda, sliding down the steeply-sloping deck. 'What we need right now is a sharp blade to cut ourselves free.'

'Even if we do, we'll still be trapped in this

awful place,' Trundle said, staring unhappily out over the mist-shrouded wasteland of the dreaded Sargasso Skies. The desolation stretched away in all directions under dark and brooding clouds. This was without doubt the gloomiest and most dismal place he had ever seen. The rotting hulks of doomed windships rose like dark phantoms out of the crawling and swirling mists, their forecastles like ruinous towers, their masts poking up like broken fingers – their rigging hanging like wind-blown spiders' webs. And as if that wasn't bad enough, the air was thick with the stink of rot and mould and decay.

The sails of their gallant little skyboat hung limp from the mast and their neat pile of provisions was now a higgledy-piggledy mess strewn down the length of the hull. The ferocious swirling winds that had dragged them off course had spat them out just as suddenly as they had sucked them in.

And things had been going so well till then.

They had sped away from the island of Spyre with two of the crowns of the Badger Lords safely stowed aboard and with clear instructions about the next stage of their quest:

You must travel to the distant and sinister island of Hammerland and seek for the Crown of Wood among the steammoles!

The steammoles! Little was known about that peculiar and secretive race. The mysterious island of Hammerland was far away from all the main habitations and trade routes of Sundered Lands – out beyond a terrible place called the Sargasso Skies. And *that* was a notorious death trap they had every intention of avoiding.